YA
FIC
RIVERA

Rivera, Lilliam,
Never look back

P9-DIY-238

S

9/20

NEVER
LOOK
BACK

NEVER LOOK BACK

Lilliam Rivera

BLOOMSBURY

NEW YORK LONDON OXFORD NEW DELHI SYDNEY

BLOOMSBURY YA
Bloomsbury Publishing Inc., part of Bloomsbury Publishing Plc
1385 Broadway, New York, NY 10018

BLOOMSBURY and the Diana logo are trademarks of Bloomsbury Publishing Plc

First published in the United States of America in September 2020 by Bloomsbury YA

Text copyright © 2020 by Lilliam Rivera
Illustrations copyright © 2020 by Krystal Quiles

All rights reserved. No part of this publication may be reproduced or transmitted in any form or
by any means, electronic or mechanical, including photocopying, recording, or any information
storage or retrieval system, without prior permission in writing from the publisher.

Bloomsbury books may be purchased for business or promotional use.
For information on bulk purchases please contact Macmillan Corporate and
Premium Sales Department at specialmarkets@macmillan.com

Library of Congress Cataloging-in-Publication Data
Names: Rivera, Lilliam, author.
Title: Never look back / by Lilliam Rivera.
Description: New York : Bloomsbury Children's Books, 2020.
Summary: A modern retelling of the myth Orpheus and Eurydice, in which
Eury leaves Puerto Rico for the Bronx, haunted by losing all to Hurricane Maria
and by evil spirit Ato, and meets a bachata-singing charmer, Pheus.
Identifiers: LCCN 2020008715 (print) | LCCN 2020008716 (e-book)
ISBN 978-1-5476-0373-2 (hardcover) • ISBN 978-1-5476-0374-9 (e-book)
Subjects: CYAC: Love—Fiction. | Spirits—Fiction. | Family life—
New York (State)—New York—Fiction. | Puerto Ricans—Fiction. |
Dominican Americans—Fiction. | New York (N.Y.)—Fiction.
Classification: LCC PZ7.1.R5765 Nev 2020 (print) | LCC PZ7.1.R5765 (e-book) |
DDC [Fic]—dc23
LC record available at https://lccn.loc.gov/2020008715

Book design by Danielle Ceccolini
Typeset by Westchester Publishing Services
Printed and bound in the U.S.A. by Berryville Graphics Inc., Berryville, Virginia
2 4 6 8 10 9 7 5 3 1

All papers used by Bloomsbury Publishing Plc are natural, recyclable products made from wood
grown in well-managed forests. The manufacturing processes conform to the environmental
regulations of the country of origin.

To find out more about our authors and books visit www.bloomsbury.com and
sign up for our newsletters.

To music,
for always saving my life

⚘ PART I ⚘

Inflam'd by love, and urg'd by deep despair,
he leaves the realms of light, and upper air . . .
METAMORPHOSES BY OVID, TRANSLATED
BY SIR SAMUEL GARTH, JOHN DRYDEN, ET AL.

If God one day struck me blind,
Your beauty I'd still see.
"ADORE," PRINCE

CHAPTER 1

Pheus

If it's a Saturday, then two things are true. First, trains heading uptown will forever be late, no matter what. Deadass. It's as if the MTA decides anyone going past 125th Street must not be worth the trouble. So what if you thought the train you got on downtown was an express 5? It doesn't matter. Right now, it's a local. No, wait, scratch that. Right now the train you've been chilling on for the past half hour has decided to not even enter the Boogie Down. Who cares if you have things to do? Trains heading uptown are bound to be cut off. It's like living back in the Middle Ages, when people thought the world was flat. The Bronx is like that for most people who don't live there: the end of the world, the last frontier, the . . . Whatever. If it's a Saturday, you are destined to do the MTA shuffle, where you figure out how best to make it to your destination.

"You've got to wait for the four or transfer to the bus," says the conductor. I wonder how many times he's had to explain this. He gives me the shrug. I give him the shrug back. What else is there to do? It's Saturday morning, and I'm bound to be late no matter how early I am.

Moms hounded me last night right in the middle of my writing session. I had the dopest hook for this new song. It sounds a little like Romeo Santos's "Imitadora," but way more sensual. I already have the first verse down. It's got the perfect combination the girls like—a little vulnerability, a little roughness. Throw in some Spanish, and it's de lo mío. This summer is going to be me working on this new song until it feels right. Shine them words until they glisten like gold.

"¿Pero dónde tengo que ir?" An old lady sitting across from me talks to herself. I feel bad. Who knows how long she's been planning this excursion?

"Tienes que ir afuera y tomar la guagua, o puedes esperar aquí por el cuatro," I say. She does a slight double take; it's subtle, but I notice it. Some people see my skin color and think, *He must be Black*. I am. I'm also Dominican. I'm the best of both worlds. Just ask Melaina and all them girls uptown I'm about to smash this summer.

The old lady thanks me for helping her figure out how to get to her stop. I start my own journey and head above ground with the rest of the sad passengers. Sometimes I wish I drove a car, blasting AC and my own music. A summer with wheels. Why can't I be about that life? I strap my guitar to my back and head out.

The second truth is, no matter the time, the sun will greet you with a "diablo, hoy te mato de calor."

It's not even officially summer, and this viejo standing next to me on this packed bus is dripping sweat. El viejo decides to provide his own musical accompaniment. He turns up the volume on the song playing on his phone. I recognize the tune right away. It's a song my pops likes to play when he's feeling melancholy. "Donde Estará" by Antony Santos.

Pops taught me to sing that song when I was six. It didn't matter where we were. In front of the apartment building where I grew up. The park. At the beach. After a few Presidentes he would inevitably hoist me up on his shoulders, and I would sing. This was when my parents were together, before she kicked him out and he headed back uptown to be with his people. I feel sad, too, whenever I hear the song. A reminder of the fam when we were a fam and not this disjointed thing.

"Yo, Pheus!"

As soon as my right foot hits the pavement on my pops's block, I hear from one of my boys. It's Jaysen. He holds a large cooler.

"Getting ready?" I ask after giving him the dap.

I met Jaysen seven years ago when we were about ten. It

was my first summer with Pops after the separation, and he was depressed. He didn't want to do anything, just stare at the wall and listen to boleros 24-7. I couldn't take it, so I headed to the handball courts, bored out of my mind. Jaysen was the only boy my age out there. I acted aloof until Jaysen asked if I wanted to play. We spent the whole summer beating all them suckers. His father works for the Department of Parks and Rec like my father did before he got on disability.

"You coming, right?" Jaysen asks. He rubs the back of his neck, trying to squash the heat. His latest tattoo on his arm is the Puerto Rican independence flag. It's coming in nicely.

"Definitely. First trip to Orchard," I say. "Not missing it for the world. I'm probably going to be—"

"Late. Bro, you always late," Jaysen says. "Isn't that Penelope?"

I turn to follow his gaze.

"Yo, Penelope!" I've known Penelope for as long as I've known Jaysen. She lives in the same building as my pops. Penelope is smart and funny. She's definitely wifey material.

Penelope pulls luggage from the trunk of her parents' car. I can't really make out who she's with. I guess it's family.

"We seeing you today?" Jaysen asks. "Am I right? You're not missing it? Huh, Penelope?"

Jaysen's been bugging everyone via text, making sure we

show up. He is relentless. Sometimes I have to tell him to chill the hell out. It never really works, though. He's a hype man when no one really needs one.

"Can't you see I'm busy?" Penelope screams back. "I'll see you tomorrow. Maybe."

Penelope turns to the car and holds the door open. A girl about our age steps out. She has a thick curtain of long, coily hair that practically engulfs her. I've never seen her before. Penelope hugs the girl, and they walk into the building.

"Who was that?" I ask.

Jaysen shakes his head. "I don't know. Penelope's cousin?" he says. "Let's hope she's fine."

"For real."

"What are you talking about? You got Melaina and every girl on this block who desperately waits for you to write a song about her."

I laugh. It's true. I got Melaina. She's mean and beautiful.

"Tas pasao," I say, laughing. "I'll see you later. Gotta hit the crib."

"Bet. See you later and bring some brews. Don't be cheap."

I head back across the street to the apartment my father lives in. I take two steps at a time and pass Penelope's apartment. She lives on the second floor with her parents. Her mom works as a secretary in a fabric company in the city. Her father is a UPS guy. It must be nice to have family around. Most of my mom's side of the family lives in North Carolina. We visit them on Thanksgiving. My father's side gets me during Christmas.

I dig in my pockets for my set of keys. The apartment smells of fresh coffee and weed. Pops never smokes in front of me. It's one of the many stipulations Mom made for my visits. During the school year, I get to see him most Sundays and holidays. Summers are his.

"Pops, I'm here!" I drop my bag and set my guitar case against a wall. I place my keys on the bowl right next to the ceramic elephant Pops got me on one of his trips to Santo Domingo when I was a little kid. I pat the elephant's head.

The living room sofa bed is going to be my new best friend for the next eight weeks. At least it's an upgrade from the inflatable bed.

"Son." Pops steps out of his bedroom. He wears jeans and the Cibaeño T-shirt I gave him on his last birthday. His chancletas hit the hardwood floors. Pops gives me a hug and a kiss on the cheek. "How was the ride?"

"You know. Same ol'."

Pops got that Sergio Vargas vibe when Sergio was at the height of his musical reign in the nineties. Pops can basically chill with anyone, but I know for a fact he still carries a picture of him and Mom tucked in his wallet. Is he still pining for Mom to take him back? Mom's been dating this bank teller for the past two years. Pops doesn't ask about him. He would never disrespect Mom like that. I want to tell him I think the guy is hella dry, like white bread even though he's Black, but I won't do that to Mom either.

I dig through my bag and pull out the Dominican flag I found at a 99-cent store the other day. I hand it to Pops.

"Nice. Thanks, son. I know exactly where I can hang it," he says. "What's your summer plan? Have you given much thought to what we discussed?"

Pops wants me to try out for a free after-school program at a music conservatory where students are teamed up with professional musicians. I love music. I do. I can feel it bubbling inside me—a new verse, a melody—and I want to jot it down. Capture the tune and share it with everyone. But music isn't everything. I'm not foolish. I'm practical like Mom. If I continue with my grades, I can step into a real moneymaking job. I'm thinking more like an entertainment lawyer. Music will not get me where I need to go.

"I'm thinking about it," I say and hope Pops changes the subject.

"The application is due in August. The after-school program is perfect for you." He can tell I'm trying to shake him off.

"I promise to give it a look before the end of the week." I mean this, although I doubt I'll apply.

"Found this for you." Pops hands me a used book, *We Took the Streets*. Pops always has nonfiction books about history to give me. I'll devour this one in no time.

"Thanks. I'll read it tonight," I say and give him a quick hug. "We're heading to Orchard. You want to come?"

"I got work to do." With disability, it's not worth it for Pops to get a real job, so he picks up odd gigs that pay off the books. Money has always been tight for him. Luckily I have my allowance, so I don't have to ask him for a dime.

"You're young. You don't want this old man messing up your day," he says. "Be safe. Don't be stupid."

I head to the bathroom to get ready.

⌐

The six-pack I grabbed from the bodega keeps my legs nice and frosty. I keep replaying the new lyrics to my song in my head. I can feel it. This is going to be the summer jam. Can't wait for my friends to hear it.

"El Nuevo Nene de la Bachata has arrived!" Jaysen proclaims as I walk over to the group. Everyone from the block is here, including Melaina and her girls. She glances over but doesn't acknowledge my presence. Not yet. Melaina is cold at first. This is her thing. She'll warm up later.

"Here you go." I hand the six-pack over, and Jaysen tries his best to conceal the drinks. Although the day is just beginning, we still want to feel a buzz. The first suntan. The first taste of freedom. Melaina's glistening skin. Summer is going to be mine.

I pull out my guitar and tune it. Pops gifted me the strings when I turned ten. There's a multitude of musical styles playing around us. Eventually the differing sounds—the rap, the reggaeton—will be pushed aside. When I start to sing, nothing around me matters. It's just my voice and the emotion I'm trying to convey. How I'm trying to capture beauty, the waves that come and go, the feeling of longing or lust.

"Stop fooling around with them chords," Angel, one of the guys from the block, says.

"Yeah!" Another one joins in. "It's time Pheus earns his keep."

"For real. It's been a minute since we heard him sing," Melaina says. "What if he doesn't have what it takes anymore? What if he sounds like Bad Bunny trying to sing a bolero?"

Melaina gives me a sexy, mischievous grin. She wears a bathing suit with a plunging neckline. Her hair is slicked back in a tight ponytail. Her lips lined bloodred. Mean and beautiful.

Those around continue to flame me. I take my sweet time. Melaina pulls away from her girls. Everyone on the block couldn't believe when she decided I was going to be the one. I knew she was mine by the way she looked at me.

"Sing to me," she whispers in my ear. Then Melaina saunters right back to her crew.

I won't sing the new song. It's still too fresh. The lyrics need some cooking. I decide on a favorite. I lean over to Jaysen, and he hushes everyone.

My fingers strum an A minor chord. A minor is a sad chord, a chord meant to pull on them hearts.

I sing the first verse to Romeo Santos's "Propuesta Indecente." The group oohs and aahs. Families turn down their radios. The girls are sexing me. The guys are looking at me too. It's the start of the summer. This song is going to be the first of many. Music is sex and games. I'm playing hard, because come September, I'm getting serious about the future.

"Otra," Melaina says.

I sing another and another until the beach closes down.

CHAPTER 2

Eury

"Eury, honey, aren't you hot?"

Titi Sylvia talks more to my hair than to me. The first thing she noted after giving me a long hug and kiss at the airport was how long my hair is. Titi Sylvia asked my mother—her sister—whether I ever cut it and how it is I haven't fainted from the heat. My natural hair is a curtain I can hide under. Mami has tried many times to chop it off or at least have it straightened. I won't allow her.

"I like the way my hair covers me," I say. "I feel protected underneath it. Almost, anyway."

I notice the worried look Titi gives Mami. To avoid any more questions, I place my earbuds in and listen to "Sign o' the Times" by Prince. The song has been on repeat ever since we boarded the plane departing Tampa earlier this morning.

There are no clouds in the sky. The Weather Channel stated the temperature will be high in the seventies with no chance of showers. Still, I search for signs of him. He's going to show up. It's only a matter of time. He'll surely follow me here. If only my hair could completely hide me from this fate. When? When will he show up? I try to steady my rapid breathing. I can't afford to lose it in this car. I close my eyes and count backward from ten slowly. Instead of this calming me down, my mind races to how I ended up in the back of Titi Sylvia's car en route to the Bronx with my mother avoiding telling Titi the truth: that I'm not well and that I'm only getting worse.

"Eury needs to speak to someone. It isn't like when we were growing up, Danaís. Lots of people see therapists now," Titi Sylvia says. "These episodes she's having are not nervios."

"Eury is fine. What happened in Tampa was just a little bump. She's been under a lot of stress to fit in at the new school," Mami says. "I've been working long hours and that's affecting her too. We can handle this. She just needs to spend time with family. That's all."

Titi Sylvia sucks her teeth.

"Don't be so hardheaded, Danaís. So many people who survived Hurricane María are suffering from post-traumatic stress. Being surrounded by family is great, but it's not a solution," Titi Sylvia says. Her tone gets angrier. "The incident in Tampa is not the first. Stop taking it so lightly."

"We've been through this already." Mami raises her voice to match Titi's. "Please, just let it go. The doctors found nothing wrong with her. Eury just needs to relax."

I turn the volume up on my phone to drown out their voices. The volume is at its highest level, pounding Prince into my eardrums.

It was Titi Sylvia's idea to have me stay here for the summer. Titi trusts doctors and hospitals and, above all else, the importance of medicine. Therapy and medication. She loves to proudly state how she had an epidural when she gave birth to Penelope and "it was the best decision of her life." She's always been very vocal about trying new things. Titi Sylvia is so different from Mami. Mami says she's too americana, too willing to accept what any man in a white lab coat tells her.

"My daughter doesn't need drugs," Mami told the doctors who treated me after my "incident" in Tampa. "Nervios, that's what you are suffering from. When I was your age, I went through the same thing. No drugs."

Mom took me to church instead. She said the repetitiveness of the mass will help calm me, and it does. Reciting prayers and lighting candles help a little bit.

How can I explain to my family that what happened to me wasn't just a breakdown? It is tied to something way more complicated. Evil. Titi Sylvia won't understand. No one can help me, not when I'm the only one who can actually see my tormentor.

He appeared when I was five years old, almost six. It would be years later when I could finally see him for what he is. But at first, he was a friend.

"Papi, don't leave!" I wail, flinging myself onto the floor of my parents' bedroom. "No! Don't go."

Papi picks me up and dumps me on Mami's lap. I wriggle and kick free from her embrace. I run to him, but he's already out the door, heading toward his car. He places the last of his luggage in the trunk. I try to climb in, but the car doors are locked.

"No, Papi. Take me with you."

Mami screams for me to come in. The neighbors look at the scene I'm causing with pity. Why is Papi doing this?

Papi doesn't look back once. He starts the car and leaves. I'm left screaming on the porch. I run back inside my room and grab the doll Papi gave me, the new one that smells like strawberries. I was so happy when he gave me the toy. It meant the arguments between Mami and Papi would soon end.

I run to our backyard and throw the doll against our tree, hoping it will break. When it doesn't, I search for a rock or a stick. Anything to damage the doll, to hurt it as much as Papi hurt me.

"I hate you," I say. "I hate you so much."

Raindrops slowly fall on my face, blending in with the tears. There is a slight rumble. I can hear thunder in the near distance. A storm is coming, like the many storms that blanket the island at the start of hurricane season. I don't stop throwing the doll against the tree. I will break it until there is nothing left of my father's gift.

"Here."

A beautiful boy my age with tight brown curls appears from behind the tree. A trigueñito with angelic features. I've never seen him before. In his hand, the boy holds a thick branch.

"Use this," he says and hands me the branch. "Go ahead."

I swat at the doll, over and over again. With each hit, the doll's face deforms. The rain drenches me completely, but I don't stop. I hit the toy until it becomes broken pieces.

"I hate him," I say, and I suddenly feel so tired. I go down on my knees. The rain now forms mud around me.

"I'll hate him too," the boy says. "We both will."

The boy kneels beside me. We stare at the crumbled fragments while the wind slowly picks up, the shower now a downpour.

"It will be hard for him to see while he's driving in this storm," the boy says. "If he's not careful, something could happen to him."

I turn to the boy.

"You think so?" I'm suddenly filled with fear, picturing Papi in a ditch somewhere, unable to get out of the car. I hate him but not enough to wish him into an accident.

Do I?

"I don't want something bad to happen to him," I say. "I just want him to come back."

"He won't come back because of what you did," the boy says. And I start to cry because I can't remember what I did wrong, but

I'm sure I did something to push Papi away. The boy consoles me by placing his hand on my shoulder.

"That's okay. I'm here and I'll never leave."

The boy says this with such tenderness.

"Eury, come inside!" Mami yells from the porch. She's been crying, just like me. "Please!"

"Your mother needs you," the boy says. "If you want, I can come back tomorrow. Do you want that?"

His voice is so soothing. His eyes are not cold like Papi when he left.

"Okay," I say.

"I'm Ato. I'll see you tomorrow, Eury."

Inside, Mami wraps a towel around me. "Eury, who were you talking to?" she asks.

"A boy."

"What boy?" she says. "I didn't see a boy. Stay inside. The storm is getting worse."

The loud honk of a car behind us snaps me back to reality. Mami and Titi Sylvia no longer argue. Their silence is proof the conversation will most likely continue later. My sweet cousin Penelope waves frantically when Titi parks the car. I continue to search in the shadows for signs of Ato. He won't come right away. He'll choose a time when I feel safe, like in Tampa. This time I will make sure to be ready. I will stay alert.

"Finally!" Penelope says. "I've been waiting forever."

"Get the luggage first," Titi Sylvia says.

"Ma!"

Penelope opens the door and instantly wraps her arms around me. My eyes brim with tears. Penelope is my closest friend even though we live so far apart. She's the only person who sort of knows what's going on.

"I missed you so much," I whisper into her shoulder. Her hugs fill me with hope.

"I know, prima. We're going to have so much fun!" she says. "We'll talk as soon as we can get away from them."

A voice calls her name from across the street. Penelope still holds me while responding to them.

"Can't you see I'm busy?" she yells back. "You'll meet them fools soon enough. They give me a headache. They're good people, tho. Let's go inside. It's too hot."

Even though she's holding me, I don't feel frail or weak. I can lean on her, and Penelope is ready to support the weight. Lighten my load, even if it is only temporary.

"Ay, un cafecito," Titi Sylvia says. Her husband, Charlie, left a sticky note with a heart drawing on the pot of coffee he made before leaving to work. "You girls hungry? Breakfast. You must be."

"Later," Penelope says.

She drags my luggage over to her bedroom and quietly shuts the door. Everything in Penelope's room is color-coordinated in a black-and-white palette, right down to the pillowcases. Her mother likes everything to be a particular style. The only splashes of color come from Penelope's vibrant clothes and the framed glamour shots of her taken when she insisted on modeling classes.

"Sit!" she says. "This is going to be your home."

Penelope opens her window. I shake my head. Without saying a word, she draws the thin curtains.

"Sorry, prima," she says. "I forgot. How are you?"

"Mami is tired of dealing with my drama," I say.

"No, she's not. She's worried. We all are," Penelope says. "We want you to feel better."

Even though we're the same age, Penelope always acts a bit motherly toward me. Perhaps it's because she thinks I'm a jíbara, a girl from the island who doesn't know any better. She opens an empty drawer.

"This is for you. And I made room in the closet. You can borrow anything you want because I intend to do the same."

Penelope was named after the Spanish actress and she hates this tidbit of information. She wishes her name was more Latinx, less white or European. We spent one summer coming up with alternative names only to find the Greek mythology behind hers. I thought the story of Penelope being the wife of Odysseus was cool. She didn't.

Penelope darts about the room, wanting to show me

everything. Her new clothes. Her makeup purchases. The latest boy she's in love with. Penelope is always falling in love.

"I've got our summer planned out. Tomorrow, the beach. The next day, the beach. Maybe there's a party. We can always hang out by the park." Her laugh is contagious. I wish I could be so carefree.

"Prima," I interrupt her. "I need to find a church."

She puts down the handful of lipsticks and tries her best to keep her concerned face light.

"A church?" she asks. "You know this family is a bunch of heathens. We never go to church."

Back in Tampa, Mami drove me to church every morning so I could light a candle. I want to keep my practice here.

"Yes, a church. Can you help me find one?"

"No problem. Let's look it up. What kind of church? Maybe stick with the Catholics. What do you think?"

"Yes, the Catholics."

"Perfect! The Church of St. Anselm. You can walk there. Easy. I've been to plenty of quinceañera masses there, and it's not a bad looking church either," she says. "Do you want to go today?"

"Yes," I say and give Penelope a hug. "Thank you."

No matter what I ask of her, Penelope never makes me feel weird.

"Cousin, are you going to tell me what's going on?" she says. "You can tell me anything."

I shake my head. I can trust Penelope, but I'm not sure if I can explain to her what is happening to me. Not yet anyway. When I made the mistake of telling Mami once about Ato, she responded by telling me to pray harder. I have, but I don't think it's working.

"Not yet," I say. "I swear I'm okay. So, the beach tomorrow?"

"I can't wait for you to meet the knuckleheads I hang with. They will love you. This summer is going to be one jangueo after another."

There's a knock at the door. Titi Sylvia serves breakfast. When I enter the dining room, I can tell Mami's been crying. Tomorrow she's set to fly back to Tampa. Mami said she has to go to work, and this may be true, but I also think she needs a break from me.

"We're going to take a walk to St. Anselm later," Penelope says in between forkfuls of scrambled eggs.

"Church? ¿Pa' qué?" Titi Sylvia says. "I haven't been to church since what's her name, the one who had the sweet sixteen mass and two months later was pregnant?"

"Ma! Her name is Gloria. Eury wants to go, so we are going."

Titi Sylvia gives Mami the look. I bow my head down so my hair covers my face.

"We'll all go," Mami says. "It will be nice before I leave to Florida."

Mami reaches under the table and squeezes my knee. I look up and smile.

———

Penelope was right. The church is only a few quick blocks away. It is a beautiful two-story building with a towering domed ceiling, historic paintings, and geometric mosaics. Parts of the building are under repair and in a bit of disarray, but I can still see the beauty in the hundred-year-old church.

Because it is an early afternoon on a weekday, the church is practically empty, with only a handful of practitioners. The service is held in Spanish and English. Mami introduces herself and me to the priest.

"It is great to meet you, Eury. I look forward to welcoming you to the neighborhood," Father Vincent says.

His handshake is not firm enough. He won't be able to help me.

After the mass concludes, I walk up and place a few dollars in the offering box. I'm sad the candles are electric and not real ones. I hate when churches go the easy modern way instead of sticking to tradition. I don't have a choice. I press the button to the electric candle and kneel down in front of the statue of Mary. Like Penelope, I never grew up in a religious household. But when you're the only person seeing Ato, you search for any type of spiritual solution that might help.

I say the prayers over and over again until Mami places her hand on my shoulder, alerting me it's time to go.

On our way back to Titi Sylvia's, Mami slows down to walk beside me. Penelope, reading the moment, walks ahead to her mother.

"Sylvia can be a bit much with her opinions, but she means well," Mami says. "Promise me you will enjoy yourself. Do fun things."

"I promise, Mami."

She grabs my hand and squeezes it.

"This will be good for you. I just know it will."

There's so much hope in her face. I wish more than anything to strip Mami of all her worries. This past year hasn't been easy for her. Leaving our home of Puerto Rico took such a toll. She really wanted Tampa to work, and it did for a while. Then came the incident at school and the barrage of doctor appointments to make sure I didn't have anything wrong with me physically. There was also the one therapist the school officials insisted I go see. Mami was furious, but she eventually agreed. So much time and money spent on doctors with no insurance to help.

"What did you think of the priest? It's a nice church," she says. "And it's so close. You don't have to walk so far. You still have the rosario I gave you, don't you?"

"Yes, I still have it," I say, pulling out the small circular rosary bead from my tote bag.

I continue to scan the streets and alleyways. It's only a matter of time before he shows his face. I hold tight to the rosary.

"We are going to get through this," Mami says. She begins to tear up, which in turn makes me emotional, although I don't want her to see me like this. I don't want to continue in this pain, and I don't want to be such a burden to Mami or anyone. I place my head on her shoulder.

"I promise I will have fun," I repeat. "Please don't worry."

"But don't have too much fun, or you won't come back to me," she jokes.

Maybe that wouldn't be such a bad thing.

CHAPTER 3

Pheus

Jaysen can't stop blowing up my phone. I was due to meet him in front of his building twenty minutes ago. He should know better. I can't rush things with Pops. Pops considers our time together a gift and won't allow me to simply bounce. Jaysen will have to wait.

"Hand me the screwdriver," Pops says. He tightens a screw on his bike.

Pops is part of a crew that soups up bikes with cool accessories and rides them around at festivals. Some of the guys have been in Pops's inner circle since they used to run around as children, catching pickup games in the park. Mom doesn't like them. I've heard her call them bums. If I look closely, I can see her point. They have grease stains on their clothes. There's a combined odor of weed and unwashed hair. I don't think they have real jobs. They're definitely not the type of men Moms wants me to spend time with. Still, they are good people and are always up to offer me sound advice.

"How long are you staying with this cabeza dura?" Migs says. His real name is Miguel, but I don't think I've ever heard my father call him that.

"All summer," I say.

"I see you're well strapped today." He gently pats my guitar case. "Ready to woo the girls, huh?"

Migs used to be a popular DJ back in the day. Addiction took him down. You can see the struggle in his hollow cheeks and the thin legs peeking out from under his baggy shorts.

"Music won't pay the bills, but it will surely keep you warm at night," he jokes.

"Leave my son alone," Pops says. "He's not wasting his talent. He's the real deal."

Pops places the Dominican flag I gave him right above the small sign that reads "Apolo," his name. I take the screwdriver and place it back in the plastic bag he uses as a toolbox. What makes him think I'm the real deal? I can sing and play the guitar. I don't think that's enough.

My phone vibrates, and I'm about to curse Jaysen out when I recognize the number.

"Hey, Mom." It's 8 a.m., and she must be on her way to work. Her boyfriend usually picks her up with a steaming cup of coffee in the car's cup holder, ready for her.

"Good morning, baby," she says. "How's everything?"

She's trying not to sound angry. This phone call is not for me.

"Everything is good. Just chilling."

"I need to speak to your father," she says.

Pops is already standing up. He wipes his hand on his shirt. Migs shakes his head.

"That's trouble right there," Migs says. Pops hushes him and takes the call.

To give him privacy, I start playing chords. The only argument they ever have has to do with money. Money for the private tutors Mom insists I need. Money for after-school programs my public school doesn't cover, like the SAT prep class or the coding course.

"I need to move some stuff around," Pop says. "It will be in the mail."

I can hear Mom arguing back.

"Tracy, I told you, I'll have the money."

I strum the guitar loudly, anything to drown out this conversation. Migs and the others take the hint and start to talk. Their action is a small token I'm grateful for.

When Pops hands me back the phone, he barely looks at me. His mouth is a thin line on his face. The wrinkles on his forehead reveal his anger.

"Pops, what do you think about this?" I play the melody

from my new song really fast. Instead of a romantic bachata, the song is now a joyful merengue.

"Sounds good, son," he says without much heart. The tools in the plastic bag make clanking sounds as he roughly rummages around. I place the guitar back in its case.

"I should head out." There is no way of getting to him, not when Pops is still so deep in the phone call.

"Be safe. Don't be stupid," he says. He doesn't bother looking up.

When I see my father like this, I see what my future might be if I don't follow the correct path. How did Pops lose sight of himself? He wasn't always like this, tinkering with bikes and smoking. I've seen the pictures of Mom and Pop when they were dating. They met at NYU when they were both studying business. He lost interest in school and dropped out right before graduating. Mom said he was trying to "find himself." When I was born, he landed for a while at Parks and Rec and seemed happy enough. Then an injury led us to where we are now. I'm all for trying to figure your shit out, but this—this is something else. Mom can't handle paying for everything, and she shouldn't have to.

Sometimes I wish my father would get a job. Any job. A weekly check so he doesn't have to hustle as much. Mom shouldn't have to beg for money. I don't know. Things would go a whole lot smoother if he worked.

I catch Migs patting my father's shoulder. Pops shrugs his hand off. Migs is right—music and love won't pay the bills.

⌒

Jaysen is doing a boxer's shuffle in front of his building.

"Why you got to play me like a sucka, fam?" he asks. "Penelope is waiting."

"If I knew she was coming, I would have walked over with her," I say, annoyed. It's too freaking early for these absurd logistics of his. "Why you got me coming to meet you first?"

"Because I need to give you the lowdown on her cousin," Jaysen says.

I wait. He's acting theatrical like he's got the dopest announcement ever. Sometimes Jaysen is tiring. I'm not in the mood, not after what I witnessed with Pops.

"Apparently her cousin had some problems in Tampa and they sent her here."

"Problems?" I ask.

"You know, mental shit." Jaysen taps his head. Does a circle with his finger.

I push him, which makes him lose his balance. "Man, shut up. Why are you starting something?" I say, pissed off. "Let's go before I take this guitar and knock you out with it."

Jaysen can be ridiculous sometimes. He has potential, we all do, but there are moments when he gets caught up in these stereotypical roles. Jaysen is smart, so it riles me up even more when he comes out of his face like now.

"I'm just saying," he mumbles.

"Let's go before I bounce. You don't know a thing about Penelope's family, so stop speculating. Damn."

We walk to my building in silence. I'm not here for people making jokes about mental stuff. It's not lost on me how my father battles depression. Everyone has a hang-up, even Jaysen with his hyperactivity. He was basically raised on cheap soda. You think I'm going to tell him that? No. I look out for him by nudging him to let go of the soda and drink water instead. Right now I just want him to be quiet about Penelope's cousin. It's not cool to talk about our friend's family like we're *Bossip*. Whatever is going on with her is none of our business.

Penelope waits with her arms tight across her chest. Her cousin stands beside her. I can see the family resemblance right away, although her cousin is not thin like Penelope. She has way more curves. Her hair is thick and long. It covers most of her face.

"Sorry we late." I give Penelope a kiss hello. Jaysen does the same. Her cousin seems distracted and doesn't really acknowledge us.

"You expecting somebody else?" I ask, trying to figure out what she's looking for.

"No," Penelope says. She glances over to her cousin. For a second, I catch the concerned look before Penelope changes it into a smile.

"This is Eury. Eury, this is Jaysen and Pheus."

I reach out my hand and Eury takes it. She has large brown eyes. No makeup needed for that beautiful melanin. A serious face, tho. No smile.

"Pheus? ¿Como feo?" Eury asks. Penelope cracks up.

"No, like fierce. It's a nickname. Nice to meet you." I hit her with mine, straight teeth and all. She doesn't respond. Not the reaction I was expecting. "How you like the Bronx so far?"

Eury stares at the corner bodega. She finally meets my eyes for a split second, then looks away.

"She hasn't even been here for a full twenty-four hours," Penelope answers.

"Welcome to the Boogie Down anyway." I tilt my head as if I am bowing to her, complete with an imaginary hat. When I look up, I notice an inkling of a grin. More than enough to verify I'm not a total fool.

Our boy Aaron honks the horn on his parents' car. Before we even have a chance, Penelope calls shotgun. We pile in. These moments are rare. Usually we are either schlepping around in an Uber or taking the MTA. I'm glad Aaron came through this time.

I hold the car door open for Eury. She wears jean shorts and a shirt, both I know are from Penelope. The clothes fit differently on her. She fills the jeans out. Can't help checking. I'm dressed in the usual, which is fine until I notice the light green shirt I'm wearing to show off my flow has a stain. Way to show them tiguere moves.

The radio is already on full blast with Cardi B's latest trap remix. Head bouncing to the tune, Jaysen is consumed with texting the plans for today, although we pretty much know where to meet. Me, I'm trying to figure out Eury, who sits right beside me in the cramped car.

Even with her hair, I can still make out that she's cute. Naw, she's not cute. Cute is for a teddy bear. She's more than that.

She holds her phone in her hand. Her screen has a picture of Prince on it. It's an old one from when Prince had straightened hair. I prefer Prince with the 'fro.

"Prince fan?" I ask.

She nods. She's not like Penelope who will talk to anyone about anything. Eury is so shy.

The car swerves and I lean into her. "Sorry."

Her jump is noticeable. There's no room in the back seat, what with my guitar case nestled between my legs. I apologize again and try my best to stick to the middle.

"It's fine."

I can hear the tilt in her voice. Puerto Rican accents are mad dope. Don't get it twisted; Dominican accents are fine as hell. I don't have a preference. I like them both. An accent makes you stand out, means you're from somewhere. You are either a step away from your home or a step toward it. Her accent sounds like old-school salsa, like the right type of everything.

"I heard Prince is Puerto Rican. He never acknowledged that side of his roots, so he's kind of wack, if you ask me." I'm literally talking out of my ass. I don't know a thing about Prince except tired ol' "Purple Rain" and how he macked on the fine Apollonia.

Eury turns away from staring out the window and faces me. She doesn't seem happy with what I said.

"It's not true," she says. "His parents were Black."

"Aight. Makes sense. It's why he got soul. I got soul too." I tap the guitar in case she hadn't noticed it before.

"Do you know any Prince songs?" she asks.

"My thing is bachata," I say. "Al estilo romántico."

"Like Romeo?"

"Yeah, but way better."

"I don't like bachata."

I cling to my heart. Jaysen laughs out loud, his fingers still tapping away on the phone.

"That's because you haven't heard me sing." I hum a tune. She's not impressed. Just you wait. She'll hear me. I've got to think of the right song, tho.

"Yo, check out that billboard. Dīs-traction. It's a new club by Kingsbridge. Now that's where you need to be at," Jaysen says. "I know somebody who might be able to hook you up."

It's hard to believe they're converting the former Kings-bridge Armory into an entertainment complex. A fancy restaurant has already set up shop with a rooftop pool and now a nightclub. Pops says he remembers when the National Guard occupied a section of the cavernous building. He also said the place has bad vibes. As for the name, they could have come up with a slew of better, catchier titles.

"Dīs-traction. Who came up with that? It's just begging for people to dismiss it," I say. "See what I did there?"

Eury barely smiles at my corny joke. At least it's something.

"It don't matter. They had their grand opening a month ago. Bused in models and celebrities," Jaysen says. "You need to be on that stage since it's definitely going to be the hottest club in the BX."

Eury has turned her attention back to the window. I try to start another conversation with her. We keep getting interrupted by Jaysen and his plans for my grand debut, a debut I haven't actually agreed to. Brother can never take a hint. Soon enough I give up trying. Instead I go over Prince songs in my head and see if I know any lyrics by heart.

⁓

Melaina has her daggers out. Strangers are not welcome in her world—especially if the strangers are of the female kind. She stands by the entrance of the beach. Her friends

Thalia and Clio beside her. I call them las Malas, because they are.

"Who's that?" Melaina hooks her arm around my elbow. Eury and Penelope walk a little ahead of us, unable to hear Melaina's tongue.

"Penelope's cousin. Her name is Eury."

"Eury?" She throws her head back and laughs. I can see the back of her teeth.

"Don't start nothing," I say. "It's ugly."

"Shut up. You love it."

It's going to be a long day. There's no way of controlling Melaina. We have never been exclusive—she sees other people, as do I. Summers uptown mean easy reunions. It's usually fun, but not when she's like this. Melaina wants to be the queen of every moment, and a new person distracts from her being the center. We join the others settling in on the beach.

"Melaina! This is my cousin Eury." Penelope introduces them.

"Nice to meet you." Melaina's expression is a mask of sweetness. A face she holds only for people she doesn't trust. "Where are you from?"

"I'm from the island," Eury says.

"What island? There's so many!" Melaina says. "You'll have to be a little bit more specific."

There is a meanness to the question. A slight.

"Girl! Why are you playing? She's from Puerto Rico, right in the center of the island where the mountains are. A mountain girl!" Penelope can see where this is heading. "Come with me. I got to buy some water. Eury, we'll be right back."

Penelope grabs Melaina's hand and leads her away to a nearby kiosk. Penelope will try her best to simmer Melaina's jealousy. The only way to distract Melaina is by showering her with compliments.

I can't today with the way people are acting out. I don't like when my friends are rude. Eury doesn't deserve it. She is a guest in our group, and we should be welcoming her. Eury watches Penelope and Melaina walk off. She seems uncomfortable. She faces the ocean, deep in thought. Does she hate us already?

To ease the awkward silence between us, I reach for my guitar. I sit on the cooler and let my fingers strum familiar chords. Before we arrived, I made sure to do a quick search online. I can improvise the parts I'm not too sure of. The song will be an offering, a way to erase the drama Melaina is trying to pull. I sing Prince's "Adore" in Spanish. I only had time to memorize the first verse. I kick off the second verse with the original lyrics.

Eury recognizes the tune right away and finally pushes her hair away from her face. Her sadness slowly melts.

No one else is around. Jaysen and Aaron are meeting others to help carry stuff. Penelope and Melaina are taking their time at the kiosk. This is my favorite thing to do—to share an intimate moment and make someone's mood change. It didn't work for Pops earlier, but at least it can here. Eury is no longer watching the sea; instead she's listening. With my voice and my guitar, I'm an alchemist.

"I never heard 'Adore' sung that way before," she says when I'm done. "It's beautiful."

"I told you Prince was Puerto Rican," I say. "Kidding."

I hit pause for a second. "You must miss Puerto Rico," I say.

"Yes." Her sadness returns and overshadows the good. "I miss it so much."

"The hurricane?" I ask.

She nods. I don't know what it must be like to be forced to leave your home. I don't wish it on anyone. There is a silence, and although silence can make others feel uncomfortable, I accept it. It's okay to let the other person find the right words to communicate. It is the same with music.

I ask her if she wants to check out the water, and she says yes. We walk on the not-yet-scorching sand. There are only a few families around. Young kids building their sandcastles. In a few minutes, the place will be jumping. I love when the beach is quiet like this. A person can think.

"Orchard Beach is no Puerto Rico," I say. I'm about to hit Eury with what I'm really good at—history. "Did you know Orchard Beach is the only beach in the Bronx? This used to be Siwanoy territory and was called Split Rock. A super religious woman, Anne Hutchinson, decided to lay claim to the land. The people were not happy. There was a massacre. So, you know, like most things, it's a decent beach created by lots of bloodshed."

A slight breeze blows her hair. The sun hits her profile like a spotlight. She radiates and I'm rendered speechless staring at her.

"Why are you telling me this?" she says. Her face is serious, but there's a glint in her eyes, a hint that maybe I'm not completely boring her. Her brown eyes are really something. It's weird how I can already form lyrics to songs just from this moment we're sharing.

"Sorry, history is my thing," I say. "What I'm trying to say is parts of Puerto Rico may have been destroyed, but beauty always finds a way of making a comeback."

"I guess that can be true," she says. "But darkness can still lurk underneath the pretty. I've known beautiful people who are arbiters of hate. Ato once . . ."

"Ato?" I ask. Is Ato slang for something in Puerto Rico? "What's an Ato?"

"Sorry. Never mind. I forgot where I was," she says. Her eyes dart frantically around. This must be a jab at Melaina and she doesn't want her to hear it. Funny. There's more to Eury than just shyness.

"Anyway, Prince, huh?"

"Yes, Prince."

Melaina's voice is loud. She is letting her presence be known. I want to keep talking to Eury about Bronx history and Prince covers. Melaina and I rarely speak about anything interesting. We keep things superficial. It's a summer relationship, and summer relationships are meant to burn up fast.

Eury bends down and unearths a seashell. When she stands, she gently brushes the sand off. I lean in to get a closer look. There is a scent of Moroccan oil emanating from her. It's one of my favorite smells, reminding me of calmness. Her fingernails are bare. Her lips, full, with only a hint of rose.

The seashell she holds has red spots and a perfect spiral.

"Pretty," she says.

"Yes," I say.

I can't stop staring.

CHAPTER 4

Eury

Speaking to people comes easily for others, especially Penelope. She went to modeling school. They taught her how to be poised and how to walk into a room wearing heels. The summer after she graduated from the Mirror Mirror Modeling Agency, she spent hours on FaceTime trying to teach me how to do the same. Penelope can talk to anyone. I, on the other hand, can't figure out what to say to Pheus without uttering Ato's name. I'm so careless. Listening to him sing "Adore" in Spanish made me forget what I'm meant to do. I have to stay vigilant.

I tuck the shell into my borrowed shorts.

"Where does your name come from?" I ask as we walk back to the others.

"It's my stage name. My real name is Orpheus," he says.

"Moms wanted to call me something kingly like David or Rion. Pops had other ideas. He said I was born to be a poet. I don't know about that."

"Pheus." I repeat his name and suddenly feel foolish doing so. He smiles warmly at me. I walk a little faster.

Penelope warned me to steer away from Pheus and Jaysen. Jaysen because he is a firecracker, popping off here and there. He's unable to focus or be contained. Pheus because everyone is in love with him, especially Melaina, who is not so much in love with as in possession of.

Melaina plants a long kiss on Pheus. When she's done, she makes sure I witnessed the display. Her arms stay interlocked around his neck. Pheus seems bothered by the gesture. Perhaps he doesn't want to be the sole focus of her attention.

I lie down on the blanket. Penelope joins me.

"Sorry about the drama," Penelope says quietly. "It takes a while for Melaina to warm up to new people."

"Or maybe she'll never warm up to me," I say.

"Ha ha ha. No!" A nervous laugh. Penelope's embarrassed by Melaina's attitude. These are her friends and it must be uncomfortable to see the way they act toward a stranger.

"He can really sing," I say.

"Aww, don't fall for that old trick. Besides, I thought you only had ears for Prince," Penelope says. "Did you see my boo? Aaron's not the smartest, but he is the finest."

Aaron laughs out loud while Jaysen tells him a story

having to do with a mean bodega cat. I haven't really spoken to Aaron, but I've seen the way he looks at Penelope. He caters to her, always making sure she's taken care of, offering her water or something to eat. Part of me is happy for Penelope. The other part wants to warn her to be wary of kindness from anyone.

I look in Pheus's direction, and he returns my stare. What does this action mean when Melaina is right beside him? It means nothing.

When Pheus sang the words to "Adore," I felt such a heaviness in my chest. I didn't expect to be moved so deeply by his voice. The first time I heard Prince, Mami was in the kitchen singing quietly to the song "Kiss." This was before Papi left us. They were still arguing, but not that day. It was such a rare treat to see Mami enjoy anything, let alone a song. Whenever I could, I would ask her to play "Kiss" for me. As I got older, I eventually discovered all of Prince's songs.

My love for Prince stems not only from how talented a musician he was, there's no argument there, but Prince was also very spiritual. In the interviews I read, he was always so forthcoming with that. After being such a sexual person, Prince found religion, and this blessing came through in his songs. Prince was telling the world you can be both: passionate and a believer.

Pheus doesn't sound anything like Prince. He doesn't even sound like Romeo Santos, although I can see why the comparisons are being made. The talent to move a person simply with a guitar and a voice. Does Pheus understand how few people have this ability? I can't stop glancing over to him.

"Who's bringing the congas?" Jaysen asks.

More and more people come to the beach. Large families and couples. The circle of friends expands. Penelope doesn't push me to join. Conversations continue without me. In between the groups of people finding space on the beach, I search for signs of Ato. My sneakers still on even as I lie on the blanket.

A tiny sparrow with speckled gray and brown feathers tears into a piece of bread, making a quaint peeping sound. This bird looks nothing like las llorosas de Puerto Rico, who are slightly bigger and darker, but I can't help thinking of them. When the llorosas are afraid, they make a screeching, crying sound, hence their name.

A young girl and boy, about six years old, give chase to the bird that flies away. The girl holds a bucket while the boy starts digging into the sand using a plastic shovel. The sun already lightening the ends of his curls to a honey color.

"Yo te enseño," he says. The girl listens and plops down beside him. The boy takes hold of the bucket and places both his hands in it. He lifts his cupped hands and sprinkles water on the little girl. She lifts her face up as if she's being blessed.

A vision of me as young as this girl comes to me. Like her, there was a time when I, too, was anointed.

Raindrops lightly tap my forehead. I lift my face and close my eyes to let the water cool my hot skin. Although I try to enjoy this, I can't stop thinking of him.

"Don't be sad." Ato appears as soon as I think of Papi. It is as if he can sense when my mind fills with heartbreak again. Papi has been gone for close to three years, but I still think of him every day. Still wish for him to return.

"Do you want to play?" Ato asks.

"Okay," I say.

"Here." He hands me a bright red trompo. Ato wraps the long string around the top's body before letting it spin on the ground. The trompo twirls so fast. It's mesmerizing to watch.

When Papi left us, Mami spent her days crying. I didn't know what to do. There was barely food in the house, but at least I had Ato. He stayed by my side, making sure I found things to eat. We picked mangos and ate them, leaving the pits on the ground. The neighbors eventually forced Mami out of bed to find a job. While Mami works, I stay with our neighbor Blanca. But I don't really need any looking after, not when I have Ato.

"Come from out of the rain," Blanca says.

We are by el Río Cibuco. Blanca said it would do me good to be outside. She planned this excursion to the river but didn't expect the change in weather. I ignore her request to take shelter. I'm too busy concentrating on the trompo spinning and on Ato.

"Do you ever miss your home?" I ask. I'm worried Ato will stop visiting me, that I will step outside my house and he will no longer be there to greet me.

Ato hums a song by Prince, the one we both love so much. "Diamonds and Pearls."

"I only think of us when we are together. I don't think of the things I miss," he says. "I can create new memories to remind me of home."

With a slight flourish of his hand, the trompo lifts up into the air. The toy turns and twists with the help of the wind and Ato's motions.

"It will be different when we are there together," he says. "El Inframundo isn't just for anyone. You have to be selected. Chosen. Do you know why I chose you?"

"No, Ato," I say. "Why?"

Ato sings the words to "Diamonds and Pearls." He sings of never running away, that love is meant for us. It's nice to be loved, to be wanted. Ato chose me.

"But what about Mami? I don't want to leave her."

He pauses. "Don't you think she might be able to take care of herself better? Then you wouldn't have to go to the neighbor's house."

I think of all those times I tried to get Mami's attention and she would just stare at the bedroom ceiling, like I wasn't even there. Even now there are times when I feel invisible around her.

I learned how to conceal my tears so she wouldn't notice. I don't want to add to her grief.

"I don't know," I say. "She would miss me."

"Like your Papi misses you?"

Ato makes the top drop to the ground. I am once again filled with sadness.

"Don't worry, Eury. I won't leave you," Ato says. "I will never treat you like your father."

And I believe him.

The little girl and boy run past me toward the ocean. Their tiny feet kick up sand.

"Right, um, Eury? Florida is basically Puerto Rico now," a boy with neon green hair says. "Everyone who left the island lives there."

"Dizque Puerto Rico isn't Puerto Rico if everyone is abandoning it," Jaysen says as if I'm to blame. "Am I right? How is the island supposed to get its act together when everyone is bailing?"

"Leave it for the next guy to fix," a girl says.

They continue to talk about my home as if they can clearly see the solution. My family's failure to stay on the island is written off as abandonment.

The hurricanes will return later this summer. Fear will march alongside and blanket the island. Hurricanes have always been part of our fabric. My mother and I have each gone through so many. We always knew how to handle the situation. It wasn't as if we weren't prepared for Hurricane María. We were. That day was different. What began as a slow build—some rain, some tossed palm trees—transformed into an unnatural predator.

They talk of my home as if they would have made better decisions if they'd been there. They have no idea what my family faced. What I faced.

"You think you are safe here," I say. "Florida isn't a sanctuary. Neither is New York."

"I'm confused," Melaina says, her body pressed firmly against Pheus like he's a wall. "Why are you here, then?"

It's an innocent enough question even if Melaina's intentions are to malign. She sees me as a threat. Melaina and her layers of insecurity.

"Category four. Category five. What does it even mean? We thought the hurricane would pass us by as so many did before. A bit of damage. Nothing we couldn't overcome." I don't look at them. I tell this story to the ocean. "The full impact of the storm hit us at 10 a.m. All I can remember is the noise. The rain and the wind sounded like the roar of waves crashing on the roof of our house. Things smashed against our walls. We thought for certain a car would be lifted up and land in our living room.

"Mami and I hid in the bathroom and prayed. Have you ever prayed against nature, against wind and rain? The roof of our house was pulled away as if it were made of feathers. In the blink of an eye, a wall disappeared. We huddled in the bathtub for hours until our neighbors found us."

No one says a word.

"Why am I here? I'm here because I am unmoored. I keep floating from one city to the next, hoping to find a sense of refuge—a lie I tell myself. My home no longer exists, and safety is a myth."

I stop talking. If I continue to speak on the hurricane, will my sentences conjure up Ato? Am I inviting him to find me here with these people?

"You don't have to explain yourself," Penelope says. She places herself smack-dab in the middle of the group so attention steers away from me. "My cousin Eury can live wherever she wants. And if you don't like it, come catch these hands."

Her friends laugh at her. The uneasiness shifts in the group. They move on to focus on something else.

Aaron turns the volume up on the radio to a reggaeton tune full of heat and lust. Melaina joins Penelope in the middle of the group. They both dance together. Their movements are innocent at first, then Melaina leads, grinding her hips into Penelope. Seductive moves meant to ensnare.

Penelope eventually sits down beside me, winded.

"I need to take a walk," I say.

She nods.

"Water break! Who wants more water?" Penelope announces. No one pays attention. Their eyes are glued to Melaina's curves, except for Pheus. He follows my moves.

"Do you want to leave? I can call us an Uber," Penelope asks. "This isn't your scene. I don't want you to feel as if you have to stay."

Penelope wants me to fit neatly within her circle. I wish I could. I want to shake this uneasiness. Even in my colorful shorts, I still bring gloom.

"Guess they were expecting a golden island girl and not this pesada from the mountains," I say.

"Ay, Eury!" She hugs me.

"Yo, wait up." Pheus and Aaron catch up to us. Aaron pairs up with Penelope. She giggles and teases. I walk ahead. I don't want to continue being the downer of the party. Pheus walks behind me. I can tell by his posture that he wants to talk. His hands gesture to the bottles of water as he digs deep to find a cold one for me.

"I got you." Pheus pulls out his wallet and hands the man at the kiosk money.

"Thank you."

"Sorry to hear about Puerto Rico," Pheus says. "I remember watching the videos and photos. It seemed unreal. I hope you can find peace in the Bronx with us."

When he talks, there is a rhythm to his sentences like lyrics with a hint of a promise behind them. Pheus is not beautiful like Ato. He has brown eyes and bushy eyebrows. His hair is in a tight fade. When Pheus smiles his dimples pop, giving him a boyish quality. A sweetness.

"What are you guys doing tomorrow?" he asks.

"No plans that I know of," I say.

"Well, if you're up to it, I can take you around the city a bit. We can see other parts."

I stop walking. Melaina still dances. Her booty shaking. Everyone cheers her on. Yet, the one person who should be her devoted admirer asks me out.

"How would Melaina feel about you playing tourist with me?"

Pheus takes a large sip from his bottle of water. Uses the coldness to cool down the base of his neck.

"Can't speak for her," he says. "The thing is, Melaina and I are only friends."

I chuckle at this. "I don't make out with my friends."

"True. True," he says. "I'm deadass serious, tho. We are not together."

"Thank you," I say. "But I don't think that's a good idea."

I am not a fool. Pheus is playing a weird game I want no part of. Melaina is with him even if he wants to deny it. He's heartless to think otherwise. If he so casually treats Melaina like that, how would he treat me?

When we return, there is a conguero playing. His face is rapturous as he stares at Melaina. His hard hands bang on the skin of the drum. Melaina controls his movements with a shake of her hip.

"Why don't you sing my song?" Melaina yells to Pheus. "What's the point of bringing your guitar if you are not going to use it?"

The others join in and beg Pheus to perform the song "Melina" by Joan Soriano. Although I don't add my voice, I do want to hear him sing again.

"I perform when I want to perform," he says. "Do you see any chains up in here?"

He raises his wrists.

"You're trifling," Melaina says. "Can't you see we're waiting?"

Pheus refuses to budge. Melaina shoots me an icy glare as if I am controlling his actions.

"I'm going to find another who actually has talent."

Melaina gathers her two friends and walks away in search of better company.

Penelope nudges me.

"That's never happened before," she says. "What did Pheus say to you earlier?"

"Nothing," I say.

When Melaina is far enough away, Pheus dusts his guitar case and opens it. He strums the guitar with familiar notes. This time, he doesn't sing the words to "Adore." Instead Pheus only plays the chords.

The melody drifts around me. What if I allow myself a little bit of this warmth? Is this even possible for a person like me? I lie back down on the blanket. If I strip the noise around me and concentrate only on Pheus, I am transported to another place where no one can hurt me.

I quietly hum the lyrics.

CHAPTER 5

Pheus

Another rush of cop cars careens across the Bronx streets. Now that the fancy new police precinct is up and running nearby, it feels as if the po-po has nothing better to do but round up the innocent all day. Unspoken curfews are implemented every time we simply want to hang. New transplants can feel safe here with us tucked away from sight. Pops mentioned how this happened back in the day when "El Demonio" Giuliani was mayor and wanted to present a clean New York. He says things are once again becoming interesting.

It's two o'clock in the morning. I haven't been able to sleep much for the past couple of days. Eury got me up at night translating Prince songs like I'm on a deadline. What is wrong with me? I bodied the song "Adore." I knew I would. And yet, she's not paying me no mind. Not really.

The ride in Aaron's car when we left Orchard was good. I felt we were vibing. She was a little more talkative. Jaysen decided to stay behind, and there was way more room in the back seat.

"You should start with this," she said, directing me to Prince's first album, *For You*. She laughed when I tried to copy Prince's trademark yell. Then she shook me with this question:

"What does music mean to you?"

I had no idea Eury was going to administer a pop quiz. I thought I was being all charming until I stumbled.

"Singing is fun. I like it," I said. "It's a hobby, you know what I'm saying?"

She frowned, actually frowned.

"What's the point of singing if you're not using your voice to move mountains?"

Whoa. How am I supposed to reply to that? She wasn't trying to son me. She genuinely asked the question, and I had no valid answer that didn't ring false. Am I being a hypocrite because music isn't the be-all and end-all for me? My voice doesn't have the power to do much but get a girl like Eury to pay attention to me. If I didn't have that, would she have looked my way? Maybe. Maybe not.

Melaina, on the other hand, sent me long rambling texts full of curses. How I disrespected her. How I should be doing the right thing and apologizing. How she might forgive me.

The next day she was back to sending me sweet messages, explaining she only wants me to succeed. She's looking out for me. I was clear from the very beginning, when we first hooked up, that I wasn't looking for anything serious. We are both too young for any of that. She's always been cool with keeping our thing casual. Melaina insisted on meeting at Orchard. She promised to make it up to me.

Penelope and Eury have been no-shows at the beach since Sunday. Four long days. I figured I would try to sing a bachata version of "Purple Rain." No doubt it was going to suck, but I was willing to give it a try. Maybe Eury would have found it funny. I don't know. When Jaysen reached out to Penelope to ask why she wasn't there, she responded with a "mind your business." Penelope is always with the mouth. With Penelope not around, it also meant no Aaron and no ride.

Melaina and I ended up sharing a cab together yesterday. She was extra nice. She even wore the tight red dress I like. Everyone on the block wants to be with her, but she doesn't hook up with just anyone. When she picked me, things turned. People started to pay attention to my music. They asked me to play at their quinceañeras, weddings. I got paid. Who doesn't want extra money? The money I spent on myself and Melaina. Restaurants. Her nails. Even this red dress she picked out at one of the Third Avenue shops.

This time, though, when Melaina and I kissed on our cab

ride home, it fell flat. I kept thinking of Eury. I kept wondering what she was doing, how she spent her day. Melaina noticed how distracted I was. She got PO'd. Told me off. I hit Melaina with the "let's be friends." As soon as I said the words, she started to laugh that deep, sexy laugh of hers. This is a game, I guess, for her.

I sit by the open window in the kitchen, my guitar in my hand. Would this song reach Eury's dreams?

Pops's chancletas hit the wooden floor. I hope I'm not keeping him up.

"Sorry, Pops," I say.

He grabs the kettle and fills it with water.

"The sirens woke me up."

Pops has been working at his friend's delivery service, taking furniture around town. They go all over the city, across to Jersey, even Staten Island. He's not supposed to be doing manual labor, not technically. I guess getting paid under the table is hard to give up. Add tips and he's making a bit of bank, enough to pay off whatever Mom wants him to pay off.

"What are you doing up?" He rubs his eyes, opens the cabinet, and places one of the mugs in front of me. Pops is a tea connoisseur. There is a tea for every mood, every dilemma. With our insomnia, he prepares a bit of chamomile.

"Hey, Pops, can I ask you something?"

"Of course, son. I may not be fully awake, but I'll still try to answer." I wait for the yawn to pass.

"Do you believe in love at first sight?"

"Hmm. I think I need something stronger than chamomile," he jokes.

Pops takes his time. It's one thing I love about him. I can ask him anything, no matter what. We've always had that type of relationship. He doesn't hold back either. When I was young, I remember this kid Oscar in my fifth grade class told me I was pretending to be Black. I came home upset, and when I got on the phone for our daily call, my father broke it down for me. That weekend, Pops took me to the Schomburg Center. He explained what it meant to be Afro-Latino.

Pops pours the piping hot water into his mug and mine.

"There's attraction, a type of chemistry between two people whether it is love, lust, or a sibling connection," he says. "A person comes into your life for a reason. You are meant to learn or you are meant to teach. Or both. There are no coincidences."

"It's weird. This girl Eury I met," I say, feeling slightly foolish for admitting this, even to him. "I don't know her, but I want to."

"And? This is a bad thing?"

"No, not necessarily. It's just. I don't know."

He laughs. "It looks like cupido got you right here." He taps my heart. "Love isn't about possession. It's a divine meeting. Respect that and don't force your way. You understand me? Eury is a person, and she's not on your timetable or cupido's."

I understand what Pops is saying. So what if I'm battling weird feelings for Eury? That's on me. I need to respect her. I'll stop trying to woo her with these chords and just get to know her.

"Go listen to el Maestro de Bachata, José Manuel Calderón, and stop trying so hard," Pops says. "Tomorrow is another day."

I hit my sofa bed. Pops stays at the kitchen table scribbling on a notebook. He's doing his calculations. How to pay certain bills. The kitchen table is usually littered with pieces of paper filled with numbers. I fall asleep to the sound of his pen gliding across the page.

———

"I'm not going," I say. Jaysen is pissed. He showed up early to my house when I texted him a no to going to the beach. I guess he thinks he can change my mind in person. It's not happening.

"Why you acting like you doing me a favor?" he says. "I mean, you are, because seriously them girls only look at me sideways unless I bring 'el Nuevo Nene.' For real though, you got to practice so when my boy calls us to Dīs-traction, we ready."

When did Jaysen become my manager?

"I'm not doing the beach," I say. "I need a break."

Jaysen stands up as if he figured it all out. He is jumping up and down. I'm glad Pops left early this morning to not witness this fool.

"I knew it. You got eyes for Eury. Man, I should have known once you started belting out Prince songs something was amiss. Even Mami fell in love with Eury. 'Why can't you find a nice girl who goes to church?' That's what she said to me the other day. Shit. I ain't got time for that."

Mass. That's where Eury goes to. Okay. She's on a spiritual trip. I didn't grow up in church. My father is a believer but not Catholic unless it's liberation theology. Priests taking arms to protect the poor is more Pops's speed.

"What church?"

Jaysen is going on. He isn't listening to me.

"Yo, what church?"

"Bro, I don't know. I mean, Mom goes to St. Anselm every single day because she always makes sure dinner is ready before she heads out. What do you care? Eury is an angel and you, you ain't nothing but el diablo."

I'm not the devil. It's true I've been a player. My thing with Melaina doesn't look good from the outside. My crew probably expects me to be with Melaina, but maybe I'm not supposed to do that.

There's a banging at the door. Penelope is on the other side, and she's screaming for me to wake up.

"What the hell," I say and grab a clean shirt. "Hold up!"

"What are you two huevones doing today?" Penelope asks. I check to see if her cousin is with her. She's not. "We are going to Central Park. You want in, or are you going to stay here staring at each other?"

"Damn, Penelope. Why can't you just ask nicely, for once?" Jaysen says. This only causes Penelope to push him.

"Is your cousin going?" I ask because I have to. I can't help myself.

"Do not mess with her. Either of you." She gets right in my face. "I'm telling you right now. I will cut your balls off. She needs no stress. I'm letting you two be around her because for whatever reason Eury actually thinks you are okay."

"I promise," I say. "I'm not going to cause her stress."

Penelope gives me a long, hard stare. "Meet in front in ten minutes." And with that she walks out, slamming the door behind her.

I get to spend the day with Eury.

Wait. She doesn't want some stink ass.

"Dammit. We are going into the city. I'm not mentally prepared for whypipo," Jaysen says as I rush to strip and jump in the shower. "I hate you, bro."

Thirty minutes later, Jaysen and I rush down the steps to the front of the building. Penelope tells us to hurry the hell up. Eury stands beside her with a serious face. How can I communicate if I don't have my guitar with me?

"Hi," I say.

"Hi," Eury says.

"Oh my god, let's go!" Penelope breaks the trance between Eury and me.

We walk toward the train station. I never get over the surge of excitement from taking the train into the city. It's as if we are playing hooky, like we're entering a domain we are not meant to enter. The train arrives, and for whatever reason, I am forced to sit with Jaysen while the girls settle across from us. Damn Jaysen for cockblocking without even realizing it.

A guy standing by the door has his music so loud. Even with his headphones on I can make out the song he's listening to is a bachata. I take this as a good sign, but I don't say a word or even hum. I catch Eury's reflection and there's a grin. A tiny one.

Okay. No singing. Be cool.

Once we reach Eighty-Sixth Street, we pile out of the train. It's only a few blocks to the park. There are groups of little kids holding hands and wearing oversized neon green T-shirts on their way to a field trip.

"Penelope, I don't want you to get lost," Jaysen says. He tries to grab her hand.

"¡Déjame!" she screams.

"So, what's up with A-Aron?" Jaysen asks. I laugh. So does Eury.

"His name is Aaron, and he's taking summer classes," Penelope says.

"Oh, he's stupid, huh?"

Jaysen gets decked. He deserves it. Aaron is pretty cool. Jaysen's only ragging on him because the guy is not around to defend himself. Besides, Jaysen should know better about calling anyone that. It's not cool or funny.

"Have you ever been to Central Park before?" I ask Eury. She nods.

"I was really young. I think we went to the zoo."

"No, prima, that was the Bronx Zoo. The first time my parents brought you here was to see the snow. You freaked out!"

Eury puckers her mouth. Then she smiles. She remembers.

"Yes. It was too cold. I don't belong in winter."

"Truth," I say. "No one does. You're lucky you only have to deal with the summer stench and crawling rats."

When we finally reach the Eighty-Fifth Street entrance of the park, Jaysen acts the fool and starts running wild across the green open space as if he's never been outside his whole life.

"Wait for us!" Penelope yells and grabs Eury's hand. I didn't know we were regressing back to childhood, but I'm in.

I run after them, dodging kids and blankets laid out for

the residents to catch rays. Parents cluck their tongues at us. Shaking their heads. I'm sure they hate seeing us brown and Black kids acting out in *their* park.

Out of breath, we drop down on the grass, completely spent.

"Remember when 'running' meant running and not running away from something?" Eury asks.

Jaysen and I look at each other. "No." We both say it at the same time.

"There was a time when we were innocent," she quietly says. "I remember."

Eury lightly runs her fingers across the blades of grass. Penelope, being the smart one, pulls out a bag of oranges from her tote bag. She hands one to each of us. The citrusy smell permeates the air.

"It is nice here," Eury says.

"Let me tell you a little bit about Seneca Village."

"Aw, Jesus! Here goes Professor Nobody Wants to Know," Jaysen says.

I get up to make my point. *"Anyway.* This land right here, where we are enjoying this orange, used to be called Seneca Village, a community founded by free working-class Blacks. Just picture it. Farmland owned by free Black folks. Alongside them were the Irish. That's right. They lived peacefully. But guess what? All of a sudden, rich people wanted to build a nice park to chill in. They started calling Seneca Village a shantytown and those who rightfully bought the land squatters. You know what happened next?"

"They were pushed out," Eury says.

"Why are you egging him on?" Jaysen complains. I ignore him.

"Cops came in and forced them out. Violence. Can you imagine? It's your home and someone decides it doesn't matter. Wouldn't you defend it?"

"For someone who loves beauty, you sure love talking about war a lot," Eury says.

"Violence. Beauty. It's all connected," I say.

"Y'all are boring." Jaysen gets up. "C'mon, Penelope. I'll buy you an overpriced soda. You guys want one?"

Eury and I both shake our heads. Penelope and Jaysen leave.

"What if it's in our nature to crave blood?" she says. There's a bright yellow wildflower by her. She plucks it.

I was taught to always be ready to defend myself. I was also taught when to back the hell down. Maybe it's a city thing. You are always playing defense, trying not to get beat or arrested or shot. Is it in my nature to want bloodshed? I hope not.

"I believe in beauty and love because I see it every day," I say. "I see it in the flower you are holding. In the orange I just ate. I see it right now."

We hold each other's stares. Damn. I want to kiss her.

I do. Does she feel the same way? I won't. This is a conversation. And yet.

And yet.

"I'm glad we came here," she says.

Clouds suddenly conceal the sun.

"I hope it doesn't rain," I say as I look up.

When I turn to face Eury, her whole demeanor changes. Eury looks at something or someone behind me, but when I follow her gaze there is no one there.

"Eury? What's wrong?"

She doesn't answer. Instead, Eury gets up and runs.

CHAPTER 6

Eury

There is a sudden drop in the temperature. Clouds form above us. A raindrop lands softly on my hand. Then another. I shift my view. Ato stands across the way. In his hand, he holds a wildflower similar to the one I now clutch. My eyes are not playing tricks. Ato is right there. He's found me.

"Eury," Ato says. He inches closer. I look down at his bare feet. The cowrie shell bracelet I gave him years ago still hangs around his slender ankle. His soles never touch the ground. Tremors overtake my body.

"I've missed you," Ato says. "It's time."

He reaches out with his smooth hand, urging me to take it.

"No! No!" I scream.

I don't know where I'm going. I just run. The rain comes down in torrents with flashes of lightning striking across the sky. My heart pounds uncontrollably.

"Eury, wait!" Pheus yells.

I won't stop. I have to get away. I push back against the crowd of people trying to find shelter. I must hide. I see a building and head toward it.

"Wait!"

Pheus yanks my arm, pulling me away before cyclists and joggers trample over me.

"Eury, what happened?" he asks. "What's going on?"

Tears sting my eyes. I keep looking back. I don't see Ato anymore, but I sense he's near. He's waiting to take me. This park is too expansive. I must hide.

"Please," I say. "I have to get out of here."

Pheus grabs my hand, and we race across the park. The rain drenches us completely. He leads me toward the street. I stumble when my sneakers cause me to slip, but Pheus quickly helps me up.

"Let's go," he says. We don't wait for the light to change. Instead, Pheus charges into traffic. We are in a video game, dodging cars as they honk for us to get out of the way. We reach the building, a modern church befitting the neighborhood. The doors to the church are locked. Pheus's breath is as out of control as mine. My hand still holds what is left of the flower.

"Are you okay?" Pheus asks.

I don't know what to say. Do I tell him the truth? Pheus looks at me with such concern. I won't bring this to him. I can't do it.

"I'm sorry. I'm afraid of thunder." If I keep my eyes down, he won't notice the lie.

"It's more than just thunder. You saw something. Someone."

Pheus tries to connect with me. I shake my head.

"It was the thunder."

He pauses for a beat or two. I can't look at him.

"Okay. Let's wait it out then," he says. "The sun is peeking from between the clouds. The storm will be over soon. It will only be a matter of time."

Pheus pulls out a napkin from his pocket and hands it to me. I use the napkin to dry my face and catch the tears running down my cheeks.

Ato is here. I don't know what to do. I want to be safe more than anything. What if it's not possible?

"What can I do to help you feel better?" Pheus says. "You can talk to me."

His words are like punches. He sounds like Ato with his empty promises of taking care of me. Pheus is no knight on a white horse charging toward a dragon. He can't help me.

"Don't worry about me," I say with more anger than I intend.

"Hey, Eury, hey." He stands in front of me. I keep my eyes glued to my sneakers.

"What's going on?" Pheus says. "I don't understand. Did I say something to upset you?"

When you've walked around with a secret for so long, the weight of it eventually becomes manageable. You easily make room for it. The secret itself feels like a living organism you feed with more elaborate lies. No, it's more like a tumor. Ato is my tumor and I don't know how to eradicate him.

This is selfish, to invite Pheus into my problems. I can't lean on him or anyone. I just can't.

"I'm fine," I say. "It was the thunder."

Pheus's phone buzzes. It's Penelope.

"Don't tell her what happened," I say. The confusion on his face continues to grow. This favor seems small, but I am pitting him against my own blood. It's not fair or right. I do it anyway.

"No. We went for a walk. Where you guys at?" Pheus reassures Penelope. "I'll call you right back. The connection here is not great." He lowers his head. Now Pheus is complicit in my lie. Another layer of guilt to add to the many I carry.

The smell of rain is replaced by his. The smell of beach, of a summery day. Pheus has long eyelashes. I return to when I first heard him sing. Even in the middle of the drama with Melaina, I felt it was only the two of us on the beach. We connected somehow. This doesn't happen every day.

"Can we stay here a little longer?" I can't face Penelope. Although she loves me, Penelope will probably tell Titi what happened. She, in turn, will tell mom. Titi Sylvia will bring up seeing a therapist, a psychiatrist, even medication. I don't want to go down that path. Mami says medication can cloud my brain. What if she's right? I need to be alert whenever Ato reappears. I can't afford to doubt what I see. Therapy and meds may work for others, but I'm scared that I might be an exception.

"We can stay here all day. Time means nothing in the summer." Pheus sits on the church steps. The rain is dwindling down.

A man with a cart filled with children's toys comes around the corner and joins us. The man dries the toys one by one. The umbrella attached to the cart was able to save most of his items. He, on the other hand, is worse off than us.

Pheus digs into his pocket and pulls out his wallet. He offers the man money, and in return, the man gives him a rainbow-colored pinwheel.

"One time when I was acting bratty, I wanted one of these. Pops didn't have any money, so he said no. I threw myself on the floor, right there, smack-dab on the sidewalk," Pheus says. "People had to walk around me. Pops waited until I had it out of my system. When I was done, he told me I was going to be in for a long, hard life if every time I didn't get what I wanted, I dropped to the ground."

He spins the pinwheel. The emerging sun catches the vibrant colors.

"What do you think? Maybe Pops should have just gotten me the damn pinwheel."

He hands me the pinwheel. I crave silliness now more than ever. If I told Pheus about Ato, how would he react? I can't even tell Penelope the whole truth. Why would I confide in Pheus just because he is showing me kindness?

It was my fault. I forgot to pray. Mami said I can calm my mind with prayers. I forgot to recite them while I ran. I need to add more prayers to my arsenal.

Maybe it was the park itself. If the park was built on hate, perhaps Ato can feel the violence. I don't know. I'm searching for any type of reason, for weapons I can use against an evil spirit. I'm ridiculous.

"I'm not one to lie to my friends," Pheus eventually says. "Especially Penelope."

"You're right. I shouldn't have asked you to. I'm sorry. There are things I'm still trying to make sense of. I don't want my family to worry," I say. "I do need help. This is true. I'm just not sure the way they're going about getting me help is working."

Pheus rubs the back of his neck.

"If you aren't talking to Penelope or your mom, who are you talking to?" he asks. "There are things, for sure, I don't tell my parents. But most of the time, I can talk to them about anything. And if not, I can turn to my friends. Who's got your back, Eury, if you're not allowing the people who love you the opportunity to help?"

If only it were that simple.

"Do you believe in God?" I ask.

"My father believes there are spirits that guide you in this life and the next," he says. "He does this mix of Catholicism and Santería and Buddhism. It's whatever works for him. My mom doesn't, although she grew up Baptist."

"And you?"

"I don't know. I think we got this life, so we better make the best of it," he says. "But hey, if prayers or churches bring you peace, then do you. What do I know?"

Pheus would never understand how Ato came to be. The only remedy I have is a belief that perhaps something out there will save me. Incantations to protect those I love. Prayers may be useless, but I have no other choice.

"You don't believe in spirits or ghosts. Demons?" I ask. Perhaps I feel braver standing with Pheus by this church. I am testing the water to see where Pheus's truth lands.

"No," he says. "I only believe in what I see. In hard work."

He pauses.

"Wait, what does that have to do with the thunder?"

His response only proves my instincts are right. He would never understand.

A woman dressed in a frumpy suit steps out of the rectory.

"May I help you?" she asks with a stern face.

"We're taking a break from the rain," Pheus says.

"Mass starts at 4 p.m. today. Please come back then."

"Isn't this church for the community?" Pheus says. "I'm part of the community."

The woman asks us to leave.

"I guess people like us are only allowed to borrow snippets of this city," Pheus says loudly. "It's only on loan, even a church."

Penelope and Jaysen are across the street. My heart has slowed back to a normal rate. The sun shines brightly. Ato is nowhere to be found.

"Thank you, Pheus," I say. My hand still holds the pinwheel.

"I got your back," he says before Jaysen and Penelope reach us. "No matter what."

My smile feels foreign. When was the last time I actually felt happy? Happiness has been unattainable for so long. But it wasn't always like this. Ato was my friend first. He was there when Papi left me. He stored my fears and secrets. I trusted him like Pheus right now is asking me to confide in him. But for Ato, friendship always meant possession.

Ato sits beside me underneath a grand flamboyán. Red petals sprinkle the ground before us. A couple of the petals even grace our bare toes. We are protected from the light shower drizzling down from above. Although it is raining, the sun still shines brightly. We sit in anticipation of a rainbow.

"There might be a treasure at the end," I say. "We should find out."

"You are the treasure." Ato taps his feet against mine. I stick my tongue out at him. He is so serious when he talks like that. It's a little silly.

There is a clanging of pots coming from inside the house as Mami prepares dinner. A few weeks ago, Mami told me to stop talking about my imaginary friend. At eleven years old I'm too old for such foolishness, she said. I'm learning to keep Ato to myself.

A neighborhood boy runs up to us. His name is Mateo. I like him. Sometimes at school Mateo will let me play with his Nintendo DS. He is always very sweet to me.

"What are you doing?" Mateo asks. His round face is flushed from running.

"Nothing, just waiting for a rainbow to appear," I say.

"Oh." He sits down beside me. Ato glares at Mateo. He doesn't like people interrupting our time together. Ato thinks everyone is out to get me, but Mateo is not like that. I ignore Ato's reaction and talk to Mateo.

"Did you finish your homework?" I ask.

"It was easy," Mateo says. I nod in agreement. Ato bristles and suddenly stands.

"Tell him to go away. Tell him you are busy."

I don't listen to Ato. Mateo is a friend. I don't have many. The kids in school think I'm too quiet and a little weird.

A fruit from the tree across the way drops to the ground.

"I'm hungry," Mateo says. "We should eat some. Don't worry, I'll get it."

Mateo gets up, heads to the tree, and starts to climb.

"Leave him alone. He's not doing anything," I tell Ato, who continues to stare at him.

Mateo straddles the tree like a monkey. He reaches a branch and slowly crawls over it, managing to stand. He stretches toward a dangling guanábana and says, "This one looks ready."

I smile at Mateo, but when I turn to Ato, his whole face changes. His eyes are completely black. And his face . . . His face appears to erase itself, like someone used a pencil to blur his features.

I shake my head. I must be seeing things.

Suddenly, a gust of wind picks up. Mateo, unable to keep his balance, falls from the tree. He cries out, and I run to him. Tears roll down Mateo's cheeks as he clutches his ankle.

"It hurts so much," Mateo cries. I don't know what to say.

"I told you to send him away." Ato's face is normal again, but he has a scary smile. Mateo continues to moan while a knot forms in the pit of my stomach.

Pheus stands before me, offering me his hand, and I'm not sure if this offering comes with a price. I'm in fear of what tomorrow will bring. Another storm to destroy everything I love. A wind to carry me away from this place.

What will Ato do to Pheus or to Penelope? I can't involve them in this. I can't.

"You guys think you're slick, but you're not fooling me. Hiding out over here," Penelope says. "What should we do now?"

"I want to go home," I say. Penelope's face drops.

If I stay indoors, I might have a chance of protecting myself. I don't know how this works. There is no book to detail what Ato is or why he is coming after me. There is only me pretending to know what I'm doing.

"Okay," Penelope says. "Let's go."

We head toward the nearest train station. Pheus walks alongside me.

CHAPTER 7

Pheus

"What's up, 'mano?" Jaysen asks.

The train is crowded, but Eury and Penelope snagged two seats at the far end. I can still see Eury from where we're standing. My sweaty hands clasp the metal pole tight. My whole body is tense.

"Nothing, bro," I say. "Everything's good."

Jaysen makes a smacking noise. "You lying. Did she turn you down?"

Penelope gave me the stink eye when I tried to explain to her how Eury and I ended up alone. She knows something went down. When Penelope asked again why we were in front of the church, I told her a story about there being historical significance to the building. Blah blah bullshit.

Eury keeps looking my way. Or maybe it's me who can't

stop checking to see if she's okay. She said it was thunder that freaked her out. The storm triggered something in her. There was real fear there.

When shit goes down like that, I know to jet. Don't ask questions. Just break the hell out of the spot and get to running. When I saw Eury's face transformed in terror, I knew we had to book. It's what my Pops taught me to do. When someone yells 5-0, you do a quick search for the strobing police lights and take off to the opposite direction.

There was an electric charge when I took Eury's hand. I've never felt anything like it before. My hands began to shake too, and it wasn't from the rain or the sudden chill. Whatever or whoever spooked her had an effect on me too. Damn. I'm not buying the story about the rain, tho. Something else is scaring Eury, and I don't know how to convince her she can tell me.

"Penelope's pissed off, yo," Jaysen says. "She doesn't want you playing games with Eury."

"I'm not playing games." Jaysen is more afraid of getting on Penelope's bad side than I am. They've known each other way longer, ever since kindergarten when Penelope snatched the ball from Jaysen and made him cry, a story she loves to bring up as a reminder of her superiority.

"Tell me something, though. I heard you broke up with Melaina," he says.

Now I'm pissed. There was never a relationship to break.

Melaina and I were hooking up. Why can't everyone see that? The way we ended last night was how we always ended it— as friends who sometimes do more. I was clear about the arrangement, and Melaina was clear about it too.

"We didn't break up because we were never together," I say. "Also, why are you talking to me about rumors when I'm right in front of you? What I do or don't do isn't up for a committee. Do you think I care what other people are saying?"

"I don't like when the crew disintegrates into separate splinter groups," he says. "We are powerful united."

This speech, tho. Jaysen has serious abandonment issues, which doesn't make sense since he comes from a huge Puerto Rican family. Then again, maybe that's why. He never likes to be alone, ever, and feels every slight. But there are no "splinter groups." I'm just not into being Melaina's prize puppy that barks whenever she drops a command.

"I'm not going anywhere and neither are you," I say. "Besides, some people don't like being in big groups and are better off one-on-one."

"You mean Eury. You talking about Eury, right?"

"Yeah, fool. Damn."

The train finally empties out a few stops shy of where we need to get off. Jaysen and I walk over to the girls.

"Let's get some slices," I say. "I'm hungry."

It's after 2 p.m. Other than the orange, we haven't eaten

lunch. Eury must be hungry too. She seems way calmer than before. I hope whatever jostled her has moved on.

"You treating?" Penelope asks.

"No, Jaysen is."

Jaysen acts as if he's mad. He's not. He owes us money from us treating him all the time.

"Do you mind if I head home?" Eury asks. "I'm not up for it."

I was really hoping we could talk. I want to try to smooth things over with jokes. Penelope disguises her disappointment with a laugh.

"Yeah, let's go home. I'm sure Mami's cooking," she says. "Who wants to eat greasy-ass pizza anyway?"

Jaysen raises his hand.

Eury doesn't speak to me as we exit the station. At the crosswalk, we separate: Penelope and Eury head home; Jaysen and I to the pizzeria. Is Eury embarrassed by what happened? I hope not. Pops's mantra spins in my head. "Be safe. Don't be stupid." I did those two things. Mom also taught me to be there for a friend, even when the person is unable to formulate their thoughts. Patience is a skill I will need to practice.

⌒

Pops stares at the television screen. He spent the past two days helping his friend deliver furniture. His hand is in a bowl of ice. I'm sprawled out on the sofa with my laptop. The opened computer tabs are out of control: *Washington Post*, *New York Daily News*, *New York Times*. So many articles detailing how kids stopped talking after the storm. Seventy-two hours of having no control, of not knowing when the storm would relent. Three full days of enduring it. I keep reading.

Those on the island went months without electricity and water. President Trump made an appearance like a demented circus clown. I followed it all, getting pissed off like so many. Santo Domingo got hit too, but not as intensely as Puerto Rico, so we helped the best we could. Mom donated money. Pops mailed solar-powered lights and generators. Jaysen's family even traveled to collect his grandfather and bring him to New York to live with them until things settled down.

After a few months, I guess we started to focus on other things. So many messed up tragedies happening here that eventually Puerto Rico got swept under the rug. Even I thought for a moment that hey, at least a lot of them are living in Florida now. Florida is probably a lot like Puerto Rico. My thoughts never came to how losing a home can strip a person of their identity. I take so much for granted. There are two apartments I can crash in, and I'm never without food. I'm only starting to grasp what Eury must have gone through.

"Pops, what's going on with Puerto Rico?"

Since yesterday's incident in Central Park, I've kept

close to home, hoping to run into Eury. She hasn't been outside. Penelope texted me to let me know that everything was fine.

"You read *How to Kill a City*? The book I got for you from the Lit. Bar," Pops says. "Same thing. Capitalists are buying up properties and privatizing them. Making sure what was once for everyone is only for a select few."

"What about the people?" I ask.

He lifts his hand from the bowl of water. His fingers still look swollen. I go to the kitchen and get him another bottle of beer. He clutches the brew with his good hand.

"Like Dominicans, our hermanos on the island are resilient. They won't go down without a fight," he says. "You have to fight for what you love."

I knew he would say something like that.

"I guess I'm thinking more about a person's well-being," I say. "What if memories of your home, what was your home, cause you pain? How do you combat that?"

He places the beer on the foldable table he set up with his dinner of potato chips and a ham and cheese sandwich.

"Hmmm. Remember your Tío Luis? The one in the army?" he says. "He was deployed so many times. When he came back, he wasn't quite himself. Every sudden noise, a car honking, sent him flying to the ground for cover. The family said it was the drugs that made him suicidal. Drugs were his way of coping."

Tío Luis wasn't technically my uncle. He was Pops's cousin. Because they were about the same age, I always called him uncle out of respect. At family gatherings, Tío Luis always kept to himself. Rarely talked to me or anyone for that matter. He always seemed angry. Pops tried to reach out to him. Get him help. Cleaned up. It didn't work. Then one day Pops called and told me he was gone. Tío Luis was buried in his military uniform and family members kept saying, "Well, at least he's not suffering anymore," while I kept thinking, *What the hell?* He should have been alive.

"Witnessing unrelenting violence can take a toll on a person with devastating results," Pops says. "To be exposed to a disaster like Hurricane María can do the same."

Seventy-two hours. That's how long the people in Puerto Rico had to deal with the hurricane. I picture Eury and her mother finding shelter in the bathroom. How would I be after watching the roof of my house fly away?

"Son. Have you gotten to the application?"

"Not yet," I say, annoyed at how he's changed the subject. The application isn't due until the end of the summer. I've got plenty of time. Besides, when I mentioned it to Moms, she thought it wasn't going to work. She has other plans. Tutors I have to see. Maybe Pops pushing me to apply is his way of avoiding paying for the tutors. I'm once again placed in an awkward position of having to appease him and my mom at the same time.

"Go get the application and do it," he says. He means business. I don't curse under my breath although I want to. Instead, I pull up the online application and start filling it. Besides an essay on how music has changed my life, I have to also upload a video of me performing for five minutes. This is going to take a bit of organizing and thought. I'll apply, and if on the off chance I get in, I'll deal with the blow of letting Pops know I can't go. I work on the application, avoiding the hard questions, until I feel enough time has passed for Pops to be satisfied with my progress.

"I'm almost done. I have to write an essay. Let me go to the store and pick up some snacks," I say.

"Go to the supermarket. Get fruit, a gallon of milk, and some aspirin. This hand is killing me." He gives me money and goes back to rewatching *The Wire* on the DVD collection I got him a while back.

When I walk past Penelope's apartment, I go down the stairs slowly. What is Eury up to? I should have at least asked for her number. All I can hear is the sound of Penelope's loud laugh. One of my neighbors says hello. She eyes me suspiciously because I'm basically loitering in front of Penelope's apartment. Feeling like a fool, I keep it moving.

The humidity hits me as soon as I walk out. Not even the storm from the other day gave us much of a respite.

"Pheus!"

I'm about to cross the street toward the supermarket when I hear Penelope yell out from her window.

"Are you going to the store? Pick me up a couple bags of plantain chips. I'll pay you when you get back."

There's definitely a bounce in my step knowing I might see Eury. Maybe Penelope will invite me in, although her parents are pretty strict. They don't let just anyone show up in their living room, especially not some random from the building. Still, things could change.

After taking way too long trying to figure out what brand to buy, I rock back to the crib. Here I am lingering by Penelope's door again like a Jehovah's Witness about to proclaim the end of the world. What is wrong with me? Even when Melaina was stepping to me, I didn't once blink about it. Swagger upon swagger. I had it for miles with my guitar ready to drop the suave lyrics. And now? I'm nervous, but I still knock.

Penelope answers the door. She grabs the bag and hands me cash. When I don't leave, Penelope glares at me.

"Thank you," she says. "You can go now."

Penelope has absolutely no chill.

"Where's your cousin?"

She steps out into the hallway and closes the door behind her.

"My cousin is still dealing with stuff," she says. "I swear

to god. I will freaking kill you if you do anything to upset her. You hear me?"

How can I convince Penelope that I'm true? I'm not trying to play her cousin or even her. We're friends.

"You know I love my guitar. I swear on my guitar that I'm not trying to roll up on your cousin. I'm just wondering if she's okay. Te lo juro."

She stares at me some more. Then she goes back inside the apartment. I don't know if I'm meant to bounce, but I wait. It's not like I can wait for long out here. Pops is upstairs.

Eury appears a few seconds later. Her hair is wet. She smells fresh, straight from a shower, which no doubt is a hard image to keep innocent.

"Hi," she says.

"Penelope wanted me to get her plantain chips, which I did, but I thought maybe you would like this too."

I pull out a grapefruit. I don't know if she likes grapefruit. I'm just guessing here. I didn't do a mango because I know for a fact mangoes are aphrodisiacs. I'm not trying to be a sucio. A grapefruit with some sugar for her breakfast tomorrow. Tranquilo.

She holds the grapefruit and thanks me. Maybe the fruit was a dumb idea.

"How are you feeling?" I ask.

"I'm okay. We haven't been doing much. Watching a lot

of TV." She pulls her wet hair to the side of her face. She has bags under her eyes. Sleep must be evading her.

"Want to listen to something? I promise it's not Romeo."

I take out my earbuds and hand one to Eury.

CHAPTER 8

Eury

I slip the earbud into my ear and wait for Pheus to press Play. The first thing I hear is the sound of the guitar. Strings being plucked harmoniously. I can almost see the fingers creating the music, setting the tone, inviting me to let go. Soon, a man's voice reaches me with this beautiful declaration of love. The singer, José Manuel Calderón, repeats the word "amorcito," and I am filled with sentimientos.

Of all the instruments in the world, the guitar is the one that connects me most to the island. The tactual feel of the fingers against the string. The changing of the chords. It's hard to explain why I'm drawn to the guitar, to put to words the emotions the strings elicit. This is why I love Prince so much, and it's why I sit here next to Pheus.

I close my eyes to envision the sweeping sound of this song

and how it's meant only for me. I let the music envelop me, feeling such yearning.

Can we stay here on these dirty steps together, listening to this song? I want that more than anything. I can feel Pheus's breath brush against my hand. Beside him, at this very moment, there's no fear. No evil waiting. For now, there's only Pheus.

I haven't been sleeping. My mind is overwhelmed with dark thoughts of Ato. The only time I felt a bit of peace was when I remembered how Pheus held my hand as we raced across the speeding traffic.

I'm falling quickly, and this, too, scares me. For so long, I have believed I am meant to suffer. After all, why did Ato chose me to torment? Clearly, I had an evil within that attracted such a spirit.

But is it possible perhaps that I can attract something else, someone else?

At the park, Pheus took my hand and ran, no questions asked. When Ato returns—because he will return—will Pheus stick by me? I can't do this alone. I have to open myself up. I'm not sure if I can, but when I'm with Pheus, everything seems possible.

"I have to head back." He points to the grocery bag.

We are both silly, standing and staring at each other as we try to say goodbye. The butterflies inside are bumping against each other, reminding me Pheus is real and what I'm feeling doesn't stem from darkness but from light. His beauty is a beauty I want. His voice I will seek.

I eventually close the door as Pheus climbs the steps back to his apartment.

"Oh my god, look at you!" Penelope says. "You have the goofiest grin."

"I don't," I say. I try my best to act normal, but I can't.

"What did he say that has you smiling like you just won the lottery?" she asks.

"Nothing. We just listened to music," I say, unable to hide what is obvious.

"Hmm, I love Pheus as a brother and because of that I trust he will come correct, but he's a guy, so I don't know. I will say I've never seen him this way before," she says. "And I'm happy to see you happy. It's been a long minute."

Penelope tosses herself in her bed. I join her.

"It's nice," I say.

"What is?" she asks.

"To meet someone new and slowly discover what they're like," I say. "This unraveling is full of surprises."

"I know what you mean. It's fun! If he does anything to hurt you, I'm ready to kick his ass, tho," she says. "Deadass."

We lie down on the bed, relishing in this joy.

"Cousin. Can I ask you something?" Penelope pauses and

I'm aware of what will come next. The inevitable question is on the tip of her tongue. "What really went down in the park? With you and Pheus. He won't tell me."

Penelope is family. She's the closest person I have in my life besides my mother. I owe her an explanation, don't I? How do I do this? Penelope wouldn't shun me if I told her the truth. If I open up just a little bit, maybe this feeling of dread will dissipate. Pheus is a sign. He appeared in my life at the precise moment I needed an anchor. I don't have to tell Penelope everything. Just a tiny bit.

"At the park, I thought I saw something. Someone."

"Someone you know?"

"Yes. Um. Sort of," I say. Even now as I say these words I can hear how ridiculous I must sound. "I thought I saw him."

I sit up from the bed. She does the same. Penelope's walls are covered with pictures of her, and I stare at the images, trying to draw courage from her wide grin, her fearless stare at the photographer. There is nothing but love from my cousin. Never once has she made me feel less than. Even the day at the beach with her friends, she allowed me room to be alone. She is the sister I've always wanted. Perhaps I can share this with her. I take a deep breath.

"The person I saw. I mean. How do I explain . . . ? He's a spirit."

I wait for her to laugh or to tell a joke. She does neither. Instead, she pulls me in for a hug. She holds me so tight.

"Eury, what can I do?" Penelope says. "How can I help?"

"I don't know."

"We need to tell someone," Penelope says. "There are people who can help with this. I don't know anything about spirits. For real."

"No!"

No one must know. Penelope wants to help, but notifying others will cause Mom more worry. I'll never forget how upset she was when the doctors told her I needed to see a therapist. When they mentioned introducing medication, Mom got up and stormed out. She wouldn't hear of it.

After the incident in Tampa, I was sent to speak to a psychiatrist at the school's insistence. He had a normal enough office. I sat in a comfortable chair, and he faced me behind a long wooden desk. There were multiple diplomas conveying his importance. The doctor said he visited Puerto Rico a few years ago. He called the island stunning. "Good fishing," he said. The doctor asked me to explain what happened, and I did as best I could. I didn't name Ato, but I mentioned how a spirit visited me. The psychologist's expression remained the same. No reaction. He quickly wrote up a prescription and handed the paper to me. It felt so clinical, as if I went through a drive-through pharmacy. The doctor barely listened and instead dished out a quick-fix solution.

How can I truly convey what I've seen to a therapist, to a white man or woman, to nonbelievers?

"Penelope, promise me you won't tell anyone," I say. "I'll figure this out."

"That's why you wanted to go to church . . ." She purses her lips. "Listen, there may be other people who know about spirits. They can give you the right candle to use and what prayers to recite. I don't know. Eury, we're just kids. I don't know how to deal with things that go beyond makeup and stupid boys."

I grab her hand.

"Please, don't tell anyone. I need time to think."

She gets up. Penelope doesn't know what to do with herself. This was a mistake. I shouldn't have said a thing. She searches for the bag of plantain chips and eats.

When we were little, Penelope believed me when I told her about Ato. She didn't question me back then. To her, Ato existed if I said so.

To offset this uneasiness, I stare at a framed picture on the wall of us in El Yunque, Puerto Rico's rainforest located in the Luquillo Mountains. We were both fourteen. If you look closely, you can tell I'd been crying.

I keep staring at the clock, wishing for time to move faster. Penelope is meant to be here, but Titi is running late. It's Penelope's birthday today, and we've been celebrating all week. We went to the beach yesterday and to Plaza Las Américas for shopping the day before. Today we'll be driving to my favorite place in the whole world. Today we go to El Yunque.

"*Eury, por favor. Pack your bathing suit and a change of clothes.*"

Although Mami sometimes doesn't get along with Titi, this week they have. I hear them gossiping about people I don't know, friends from their childhood. It's nice seeing Mami enjoy herself and not worry about things.

"*Make sure you close the window,*" *Mami says.* "*It looks like it's going to rain.*"

Before I get to the window, I text Penelope and ask what's taking her so long. She responds with a picture of herself sporting the new lipstick she bought at the Plaza. You can't rush me, *she texts.* I'm a woman now.

Just hurry up, *I respond.*

When I turn the latch on the window, I notice Ato sulking outside. Unlike my mother, Ato hasn't been happy with the family visitors. He says I've been ignoring him. Truth be told, I don't have it in me to be with Ato like before. Penelope says I need to go out more. Go to dances. Eat pizza with friends. And I try. But every time I do, Ato gets mad.

I finish packing my bag and wait outside for Penelope to arrive.

"*You're leaving me again,*" *Ato says.*

I don't dwell on the tone he uses with me, although it is grating. I'm tired of being accused of being a bad friend.

"*We'll be back later,*" *I say and check my phone.*

"*You're not even going to invite me.*"

"It's Penelope's birthday," I say with a bit of my own attitude. "It's not about us."

Ato sits by me. "It's always about us."

Qué pesado. There's never any room for anyone else. I can understand Ato's jealousy with my school friends, but Penelope is family. It's always the same arguments. While I feel I'm changing, Ato just wants everything to remain exactly the same as when we were five years old.

"You can't go." He's being ridiculous.

A car pulls up the driveway. I scream to Mami to let her know they've arrived. "Ato, try to understand," I say and run to Titi's rental car. I leave him and his brooding self. I won't let Ato ruin today. I watch him from the rearview mirror as we depart.

In the back seat, Penelope tells me all there is to know about eyeshadow. When Mami isn't looking, she dabs a bit of shimmer on my cheeks and eyes.

"Get that Rican glow!" she says.

We reach Río Grande in no time. When we start the drive up the winding Luquillo Mountain road, I stretch my hand out the car window to try to touch the leaves. "Doesn't el Cuco live here?" Penelope asks. I laugh at her. "No, but Toño Bicicleta does with el chupacabra." Penelope tells me to be quiet, but she looks around the dense foliage with a tiny bit of apprehension.

We don't come to El Yunque as often as I want to. The first time I visited it was for a school field trip when I was eight, and I fell in love with it. There is something magical about the rainforest. It's so quiet and peaceful here, even with the tourists. You feel as if you've entered another world. While Titi and Penelope pose for pictures, I walk ahead toward the falls. It's amazing how in only a few steps, the foliage can immerse a person. Soon my family's voices drown and I hear only the fantastical sounds of the rainforest. I spot the bromelias and yellow heliconias. Their colors stand out against the lush greenness. The flowers are gorgeous, but I'm searching for my favorite birds, the llorosas.

"There you are," I whisper. I don't want to startle the brown speckled bird up on the branch. In my bedroom I have pictures of the birds on my wall. They say the llorosas sound like people crying. Maybe it's because of this I feel so connected to them—because they are as sad as I am.

"No estés tan triste, pajarito," I say quietly. The llorosa stares down at me.

"I told you not to go."

I turn around to see Ato before me. Why is he following me? I clench my jaw and feel my whole body tense up. El Yunque is my place. Him being here is a violation, as if I can never have any fun without him.

Ato looks up at the llorosa. I break into a cold sweat.

"Don't, Ato," I say. "Leave the bird alone."

"You've made me do this," Ato says before his eyes go dark, and I stop breathing. The llorosa cries out, sounding humanlike in its shriek, then drops to the ground.

"No! Why, Ato, why?"

Penelope soon finds me. I can't stop crying. And Ato? Ato just stands there. No one can see him. Not Penelope. Not Mami. Not Titi. I can't tell them what happened. All I can do is fall to the ground beside the motionless llorosa and weep.

"Ay, pobrecita," Penelope says. "Pobre llorosa."

There is an invisible line drawn that places believers on one side and nonbelievers on the other. I wish Penelope could see there is more to this world than the obvious. Now that I've uttered Ato's name publicly, I must find a way for Penelope to understand the gravity of my situation and how important it is that no one else find out.

This fight is my own, and the adults in my life will never fully grasp the destruction Ato can unleash. Penelope has to trust me.

"Okay. We will figure something out," Penelope says. "We always do. Right?"

Her optimism isn't quite there but it's more than enough. I can hold on for a little bit longer.

A knock on her bedroom door startles us.

"Eury, your Mom is trying to call you," Titi Sylvia says. "Come and talk to her on my phone."

"Please," I whisper to Penelope before leaving.

"Are you eating?" Mom doesn't say hello, she just goes straight into questions when I get on the phone. "I want to make sure you are eating."

"I am," I say. "How's work?"

When we moved to Tampa, Mami had a hard time finding a job. While she applied to countless office positions, she worked taking care of a newborn for this Cuban couple. The hours were long and it didn't give her much time for anything. I spent those early weeks in Tampa alone in the house. Mami didn't have time to figure out why I was so quiet. Why I preferred the indoors or why my whole body shook whenever it rained. Instead, she told me to rest. To take naps. To pray.

"Eury, are you trying?" she asks.

The question is so loaded. Are you trying to fit in? Are you trying not to be so awkward, to not make others feel uncomfortable?

"Yes, Mami. I'm having a good time," I say. "I'm resting when I get too excited."

"Ay, qué bueno," she says and I can hear it in her voice, the sense of relief that perhaps she was right, that the Bronx might do me some good.

"I can't stay long on the phone. You know how this woman is," she says. When I had my episode in Tampa, the lawyer Mami now works for got so annoyed. She didn't like how Mami had to miss work to take me to appointments. The lawyer kept wondering why Mami couldn't ask family to take care of me. "The church is so nice. I think you are going to like it there."

"Yes, Mami. We went to the beach and the park. Penelope's friends are nice. I'm trying."

"¿Y los nervios? Anything?"

"No, ningún ataque de nervios," I say. "I'll call you tomorrow. Don't worry."

"I'm so glad. Okay, call me. I love you."

This is what she wants, for me to feel good. For once, I can offer her a bit of relief. It's possible for me to get out from under this veil of darkness.

"Bendición, Mami. I love you too."

I hang up. The load is becoming lighter to carry. I can feel it. Telling Penelope was scary to do, but with her, I can manage this, and maybe I will find the courage to let Pheus in as well. It's a step, a small one.

I stand by Penelope's room. Titi Sylvia is still in there talking to her. I hear my name.

"She had another episode," Penelope says.

"Ay, Dios mío," Titi Sylvia responds.

"Ma, she said she saw a spirit."

"Danaís told me she was seeing things in Tampa. That she saw a spirit during class and had a meltdown. That poor girl," Titi says. "I wanted Danaís to send her here so she can get professional help, but my sister is so stuck in her ways. Now this. Enough is enough."

I tiptoe quietly to the bathroom and close the door. I feel like throwing up. Penelope told her mother, even though I begged her not to. I thought my cousin would understand how hard this is for me and respect my wishes. Even allowing her a glimpse of what I'm dealing with wasn't easy. I put myself out there. I should have known better. This life was meant to be dealt with alone. Penelope betrayed me. I'm completely on my own.

My face glistens from the heat. The bags under my eyes keep getting worse. There is something to this life I'm not getting. How do I continue to love my cousin when she broke my trust?

I'll go back to pretending everything is fine. Mami has been through enough, and it's all my fault. From now on, no one will see what is happening to me. I will show no fear. No anxiety. I'll be an actress. This is what I will do.

Penelope and Titi mean well. I know they love me, but their love is not enough. There was a time when I thought Ato loved me too. He was there when Papi left. Then one day Ato's love had a price attached to it.

No. I can't trust anyone.

I splash cold water on my face. When I hear Titi Sylvia in the kitchen, I leave the bathroom.

"How's your mom?" Penelope asks.

"She's fine," I say and turn to study the Weather Channel. Penelope doesn't notice the change. No one will.

CHAPTER 9

Pheus

Jaysen smacks the handball against the graffitied wall. It's 9 p.m. and there's no letup to the scorching heat. I sit against the fence wondering what Eury is doing. Again.

"Yo, she said she didn't like bachata," Jaysen says, hitting the ball. "Maybe she thinks you suck."

"It's not about bachata. I don't care if she doesn't like my music." I run up on the ball before Jaysen gets to it. I can feel the sting on the palm of my hand. "I kind of like that she's not a fan. Makes our conversations way more interesting."

The moment Eury and I shared in the stairwell may have been brief, but it still lingers in my thoughts. When did I become so wrapped up over a girl I just met? I smack the ball again.

"Can we change the subject?" Jaysen says. "For real, tho,

you're a broken record. Eury this. Eury that. Bro, concentrate. We have serious business to tend to."

Jaysen wants to talk about my music and playing at the new club. Dīs-traction is by far the dumbest name for a nightclub. But his connection came through and they want to try me out.

"You need a full-on band," he says. "It's the only way we can do this. Make you look legit."

I've fooled around with other musicians during unexpected jam sessions at the beach. Strangers show up. Old-school players join in. There have even been times when a white boy thinks he can wiggle in with his congas and take over. When that happens, we shut it down real quick.

"Who are we going to get to play?" I ask.

Jaysen rattles off names of decent musicians who won't flake or ask for money.

"If we do this, we got to do it right," I say. Concentrating on the club date is an easy distraction from my Eury woes. "How much time are they giving us?"

"Three freaking songs. You better pull them out. They better be crisp so the owner will want to hire you for the summer," he says, grabbing the ball for a sec. "Our whole crew will be there. It will be all ages. My connect says they want to experiment to see if they can capture the youths."

"Capture the youths" like we are some sort of exotic animal. Music is a business. The owner wants the club filled with kids willing to spend money on overpriced drinks. Picture that, here in the Bronx, where money is always tight for most people. This isn't Fordham Road, by the university, where you got the college students rolling in the green. Then again, if you take a good look around the block, more and more hipsters are filing in.

"Think Penelope will go?"

Even I know I sound like a baboso. Pining for Eury like a weirdo.

"Chacho. She got you good, didn't she?" Jaysen says, shaking his head. "I don't get it."

"You ever met somebody and started lining up conversations you want to have with them?" I say. "Like, you have an ongoing agenda of topics you want to share? There are hundreds of questions I want to ask Eury. I just want to get to know her."

Jaysen wipes the sweat from his forehead with the back of his hand.

"I used to think I was the sidekick in this duo. Now I'm questioning my whole life." Jaysen's laugh echoes off the walls of the empty schoolyard.

He's right. I'm sounding desperate. Damn.

Melaina strolls into the yard with las Malas, Clio and Thalia, each slurping on a coquito. Clio grew up in the Patterson Projects. She's the youngest of five kids. Her mom works in the school cafeteria, which means Clio's fridge is always filled with them tiny milk containers her mom heists from her job. Even though we've teased Clio about it, whenever she offers us chocolate milk, we drink it like it's the elixir of the gods.

The basement in Thalia's house is where most of us hang during the winter months. Her family's house parties are notorious. There's a DJ, catered food, the works. It was at their party last year that Melaina and I hooked up. Thalia's family insisted I sing. The few tragos I took from the Mamajuana bottle got me so lit I could barely see straight. My lips were loose. I sang one bachata after another. Thalia's family couldn't get enough of it. Couples were grinding in that basement like they were auditioning to appear on *Sábado Gigante*. But not Melaina. Her usual partners were there, the older boys with money. The ones who pick her up in their cars and take her to places I can never afford. Still, she watched only me. Drunk or not, I knew where the night was heading.

"Hi," Melaina says. She wears cutoff jeans with the pockets hanging out and a tight tank top. Her box braids are styled to the side. She has a dancer's body—long neck with a curvy back.

"What's up?" I take the handball from Jaysen and lazily throw it against the wall.

Jaysen rolls up to Clio. He's been trying to chat up Clio for the longest. Them girls are not easy. They play and party hard. Jaysen should stick to handball because Clio, like

Melaina, will destroy him. He tries to get her to give up some of her coquito. Clio refuses. They keep doing this. Even with the hate she emanates, Clio also shows a bit of love by pressing her shoulder against his. Jaysen will keep trying to win her over.

"Win her over." Guys always trying to win over a girl like she's a prize. As if this life is a contest. Manipulate people's feelings to get them to press up against you or to share sweet coquito. I've done it countless times. Where did I learn this? Not from Pops. He isn't down with that kind of life. He taught me to respect and treat others as equal. And yet, here I am playing the game. Trying to manipulate Eury to see I'm a good guy; how different am I from the others?

Eury is not a prize. She can do what she wants, like me.

Melaina's eyes are rimmed with black eyeliner. Her nails are outlined with sparkling gems. Those claws are known to draw blood. If Melaina scratches you, it's practically a souvenir. Instead of a hickey, a scar to mark you.

"Bring all your fly nenas to the club," Jaysen says. "We got to support our boy Pheus."

He pats me on the back.

"Maybe," she says.

Melaina will be there, and she'll be the hottest girl in the club. No doubt.

"It's going down next Monday. Mark your calendars."

There's much to do. Three songs to prepare. Of course,

I'mma hit the crowd with a Romeo Santos to pay my respects to those before me. Then do a cover of a contemporary artist in Spanish. Should I sing a Prince song? I liked the way "Adore" came out. Would Eury be there? Would she like that? She might not even show up. I need to stop tripping.

Melaina offers me some of her coquito. I take a bite. It's sweet, with chunks of coconut—the perfect thirst quencher.

"Where's Penelope and the church girl?" Melaina says. "I mean her cousin."

Melaina is jealous. I've never seen her this way. It's kind of funny. Does Melaina see the same thing I see in Eury? We are both witnesses to Eury's pull. I want to see Eury again, and Melaina knows it.

"She goes to church every day. Como una monja," Thalia adds. "She's going to heaven, unlike us."

"I don't believe in heaven. We got only this," I say. "This moment right here. This earth. Dassit."

"Then that makes you an anarchist," Jaysen says.

"No, stupid, that makes him an atheist," Melaina says. "I don't see how you can be an atheist. Who made this world? Who made you?"

She pokes me with the tip of her nail. I've had this conversation before with Pops. He's given me countless books to try to change my mind. Books on Buddhism, reincarnation. Pops even hits me with Caribbean folklore. The Bible is filled with great stories too. Is any of it based on truth? I'm coming from a place where if I don't see it, I don't trust it. The person writing the narrative is the person in power.

"I like to keep my feet on the ground, know what I mean?" I say.

"I bet you church girl wouldn't be happy to hear that."

"Stop calling her church girl. Her name is Eury," I say with anger.

Melaina is quick to respond. "I can call her whatever the fuck I want," she says. "Are you her man or something? Stop protecting a girl who doesn't give two shits about you."

She's wrong. Eury isn't coldhearted. I can see past the sadness. I could see a tiny bit of happiness yesterday when we tried to say goodbye, goofily staring at each other.

Melaina wants to argue about this. I don't need to defend Eury. She doesn't need me to.

"I'm out," I say. "Later."

Melaina drops her attitude. She's disappointed I don't want to engage in a war of words with her.

Melaina lives with her mom. Her father bounced early on. She's never met him. Her mother is a manager of a department store up on Third Avenue, and Melaina is a replica of her.

One night we were chilling in Thalia's basement. We had the corner of the sofa to ourselves. It was late, and the lights were dim, and I guess in the dark, Melaina felt courageous.

She went on to tell me how much she wished her father were around.

"She hates me." Melaina said her mother blamed her for being single. In the darkness of the basement, her eyes glistened as if she were on the verge of tears. The hard exterior isn't always on. I just wish Melaina would let the softer side of her show more often.

"Yo! What about the gig? We haven't finished talking!" Jaysen yells.

"Text me, bro," I say.

I love my friends. I love my boys. I even have cariño for Melaina. But if the circle we've created is not allowed to expand to include a new person, what's the point?

⁓

The apartment is empty. Pops had a late drive to Boston. He said he would spend the night to avoid any accidents. I guess the extra hours of work paid off enough for Moms to stop calling him about money.

Pops's pride and joy is his wall of towering bookshelves. He once said you can tell a man's worth by the number of books he owns. I guess this means Pops is overflowing with riches because ever since I can remember I was never without a book within reach.

My friends got me thinking about spirituality since last

night's interaction. Church girl. So what if Eury found the answer in religion? It must be nice to trust in something greater. Moms taught me if you work harder than the person next to you, you might make it. "Your skin color means you can't fail, means you are not allowed to make a mistake."

I pull out Pops's copy of the Bible. The only story I've always liked is the book of Revelation. The Bible transforms into comic book epic-ness with the Four Horsemen of the Apocalypse. Genesis is a good one too. How these people were living the high life and all of a sudden, God rained down on them. The most intense part was when Lot's wife looked back after God told her not to and she turned into salt. The Bible bugs out. Like, you better listen to God. If homeboy says don't look back, don't look back.

Hi. It's Eury.

I do a double take. Eury is on my phone right now, sending me a text as if the power of reading the Bible summoned her.

What's up? I type and wait eagerly for her to respond. *You want to hang out tomorrow? Maybe grab a slice or something.*

There is the longest pause. It might only be a few minutes, but I'm staring at the phone thinking it's broken.

I hope you don't mind I got your number from Penelope, she says. *I have a favor to ask. Will you walk me to church?*

Tomorrow is Sunday. Of course she would be going to church.

You don't have to stay for mass, she says.

I'm going to do it, but her request also got me wondering. Why isn't she asking Penelope to go with her? Are they on the outs?

Sure. What time?

9 a.m.

Ouch. Early mass. Summertime is not meant for early mornings. And me, I'm bound to be late. There's no way I'm going to be able to get to her on time.

No problem, Eury, I say. *I'll meet you downstairs at 8:15 a.m. Is that cool?*

Thank you.

There's another long-ass pause. Communicating via texts makes everything cold. I can't see her reaction or gauge if there is more to this ask.

I'll see you tomorrow then, she texts.

I set my phone's alarm, which I'm scared I'm going to ignore. I set a small radio alarm as backup. Too bad Pops is not here because if he were, he would wake my ass. I don't want to mess up. Eury wants me to go to church with her tomorrow. I want to do right. Can't have my notorious lateness ruin this.

I hit the sofa bed early. But I can't really sleep.

CHAPTER 10

Eury

Pheus is nowhere to be found.

I wait at the street corner, far away from the apartment building and Titi Sylvia's prying eyes. When I told her I didn't want to go to the beach with Penelope and instead wanted to attend mass, she insisted on joining. It took everything to convince her I could go by myself. Titi Sylvia has been watching me like a hawk. I feel like a fish in a bowl being stared at by humans as they tap on the glass to get my attention.

A cat slinks out from behind two garbage cans and meows. I already checked the weather on multiple channels. Summer sprinkles is what the forecast predicted. I can't wait for him any longer. Texting Pheus was an impulsive act. I felt so alone after Penelope's betrayal, and when she wasn't looking, I found his number. I regret it now. He's not coming, and I feel stupid for even thinking he would.

Penelope sensed something was amiss between us. I didn't confront her. There's no point in doing so. She did what she did, and I'm sure I'll suffer the ramifications from her actions soon enough. Secret conversations in regards to how best to take care of Eury and her bungled-up mind are surely being hatched. For now, I need to protect myself. This means attending church and hoping the prayers will help me in some way.

Pheus is not showing up. I need to go.

The walk to the church isn't far. This is the first time I do it on my own. As always, I scan the buildings and the sidewalks for any signs of Ato. I examine the gray sky for clouds. I'm so nervous and angry for falling into this trap, for allowing myself to trust Pheus and Penelope, even for a second.

There is a sudden rush of footsteps behind me. My heart thumps.

"Eury! Wait up!"

Pheus is out of breath.

"Sorry I'm late."

I keep walking. The mass will begin in fifteen minutes. Where I sit is important. I need to be by the exits. I want to also be by a window so I can check any change in the weather.

"I don't have time to waste," I say.

Pheus picks up the pace to join mine. We walk in silence. When we enter the church, I'm amazed at how packed the place is. It's unlike the other days when there are usually just abuelas clanking their rosary beads in prayer.

"You don't have to stay," I say. I managed to walk most of this on my own. Maybe I can handle the rest without him.

"I promised I would take you here and I can walk you back," Pheus says. "It's not a big deal."

"Let's sit here then." I pick a pew close to the side entrance of the church. There is a window left slightly ajar. The opening is more than enough for me to see through. When I feel secure in my surroundings, I finally pay attention to Pheus. He smacks his hands together as if he's about to clap. He's nervous. My coldness over his lateness weighs on him.

"Hey, Eury. I'm really sorry I got to you late," he says. "It won't happen again. I'll make sure of—"

"Do you ever go to church?" I ask, not wanting to dwell on his misgivings.

He shakes his head. "Naw. This is new."

"You don't mind coming, then?"

"I heard they serve bread and wine, right?" he says. "Can't be that bad of a place."

When Pheus jokes, his eyebrows go up. I can imagine him as a little boy. How mischievous he must have been. He was probably a handful. A little boy craving attention, ready to perform in front of an audience. Pheus is usually so self-assured, but he doesn't have his guitar now to give him confidence.

"I find the smell of incense calming," I say. "The scent feels so rooted in history. I'm transported to another time and place. I'm not even sure exactly where."

Ritual is what I love most about attending mass. Sit up. Kneel. Call and response. It wasn't long ago when attending mass was new to me too. Mami found a church close to the house we rent in Tampa. She said attending would help quell my intense thoughts.

"If attending mass and praying to a guy on a cross helps people, I don't see it being a problem," he says. "What upsets me is when people believe god or praying will pull you out of poverty or what have you. Nothing can help but this right here."

He shows me his hands. Pheus thinks praying is a sign of weakness. Titi Sylvia would probably agree with him.

"There's power in words," I say. "I want to believe I'm beloved, that my prayers are being heard."

"Sure, I guess," he says.

He has doubts, but I don't have a choice. My religious pleas are my only hope for any type of protection from Ato. I need to believe.

I help Mami with the shopping bags. In the corner of my eye, I see Ato lurking in our backyard. I ignore him.

"Eury, do we still have the candles from last time?" Mami asks. I search underneath the kitchen sink, where we store things, and

find the candles nestled inside a pot we no longer use. I take them out and find lighters and boxes of matches. I place a candle and matches in each room.

Hurricane Irma is due to hit Puerto Rico tomorrow morning. It's already starting to rain. I switch the television on so we can listen to the news. We've been out all morning making sure we have enough food and water. If there is a blackout, we have our candles. We've been through this before.

"I'm going to put the chairs away," I say. Mami continues to get things ready inside.

Before I leave, I take a deep breath. After the incident in El Yunque, Ato went away for a few months, and that was fine with me. I didn't want anything to do with him. When Ato returned, he apologized, but things were unsolvable by then. Although I still care for him, I keep my distance. I try to safeguard myself from his rage.

I stack the plastic chairs one on top of the other. Ato just stands there, watching.

"I got you something," he finally says.

"You don't have to give me a gift," I say. "It's not my birthday." I grab the chairs and store them in the garage. I go back to do the same for the side tables when I see the gift placed in the center of one of them. It's a jewelry box with an illustration of Prince on top. With a quick flick of his wrist, the lid opens and a familiar tune plays.

"Remember how we used to listen to this song? I know it's one

of your favorites," Ato says. The jewelry box plays an eerie instru-
mental version of Prince's "Adore." I find the music disturbing. He's
tainted my song by trapping it in a tacky box. I close the lid and
try to mask my discomfort.

"I better go inside," I say. Ato reaches his hand to me, but I
don't take it.

"We're going to be together soon," he says.

He makes these declarations every once in a while. I don't ask
him what he means by them anymore. I fake a smile and walk
back inside the house. I store the jewelry box deep in one of my
drawers, out of sight. I don't know how to handle Ato anymore.
I grow more and more fearful of him.

At night, I lie in bed and try to sleep. Every time I interact with
Ato, I notice the patterns to his anger and his obsession with me.
This can't go on. I close my eyes and press my hands together. I've
never been one for church or prayers, but I have to do something.

Tonight I will ask for the courage to break free from Ato.

The next morning, when Hurricane Irma lands on the island,
Ato is nowhere to be found, and I think, Maybe my words
finally worked.

Father Vincent approaches each pew, greeting families
with a hearty handshake. There have been times when I lin-
ger long after the mass has concluded. Father Vincent allows
me those solitary moments so I can meditate and try to quiet
the hectic pace of my mind.

"Ah yes, el Nuevo Nene de la Bachata," exclaims the priest. Pheus acts modest. "How's your father doing?"

"He's good," Pheus says.

"This is perfect timing. Perfect. We need new singers for the choir. It's mostly young kids. You don't mind picking up the guitar, do you?"

"Actually, I don't know any of these songs," Pheus says, nervously laughing.

"It's easy chords. The song is right here." Father Vincent opens the songbook and points to what they'll be singing.

The priest has placed his hand on Pheus's shoulders, leading him to the front of the church. Pheus mouths *help* but Father Vincent will not let him go. I laugh. It's one thing to be dragged to church at such an early hour, but now he must perform. Someone hands Pheus a guitar. He tunes it while also trying to memorize the first song.

I take a deep breath. I'll be fine. More families enter wearing their Sunday best. Mass is about to start. From where I sit, the sky is still very gray. I exhale.

An older lady with a warm smile sits next to me. I recognize her from the weekday masses I attend. Her name is Doña Petra. Of course, she knows Penelope and Titi Sylvia.

"Qué calor," Doña Petra says. She pulls out a sequined fan. The church is extra stuffy today. The air feels so heavy. Doña Petra drops the fan down by me and gets up to open the window even wider.

"Ah, allí está Orfeo," Doña Petra says when she returns. "¿Él es tu novio?"

Of course she would know Pheus too. I respond with a no, but my grin is hard to conceal.

Pheus is placed amid the choir of young kids. He seems so at ease. The choir director, who also strums a guitar, motions for Pheus to begin. The song, "Vienen con Alegría," is a welcome song, happy and cheerful. The choir is strong. They know what to do. After the first verse, they stop singing and allow Pheus to take the reins. The acoustics in the church project so far. His voice is sonorous and so soothing. Everyone—the priest, the churchgoers, even Doña Petra—is enraptured.

Pheus pulls a handkerchief from his back pocket and wipes his forehead. I mime a quiet clap for him. He does a slight bow and flashes his dimples. This is where Pheus truly shines. When Pheus is in front of an audience, it's as if he becomes another person, a more heightened version of himself.

Father Vincent stands by the podium. He raises his hand to signal to everyone mass is about to begin.

Toward the back of the church, a baby starts to cry. It's a guttural wail made all the louder because of the sudden silence. Another toddler joins in. A boy throws himself on the floor and begins to kick and scream. Throughout the church, babies fuss and bellow. Crying children are everywhere, as if they all caught the same tragedy. Even Father Vincent is unsure how to proceed.

Pheus has a look of surprise. More kids join in. They weep in unison.

And I realize what this is. I know what's coming.

I look out the open window. Raindrops hit the windowsill. The babies will not stop screaming.

I see him. He's here.

Ato.

Outside, the wind picks up and rattles the stained-glass windows. I can't hear a damn thing. The children won't stop crying. The hairs on my arms stand. Something is not right. I look to Eury, and her face tells me all I need to know.

I drop the guitar and run to her. She stares in fear toward the open window. I don't see what she's seeing.

"Ayúdala," the old lady says, urging me to help her.

"Hey, Eury!" I grab her shoulders. She finally sees me. The rain enters the inside of the church from the window.

"He's out there," Eury says.

"Who is? Who's trying to get to you?"

She can't say, so I do what I do. I grab her hand and move away from the crowd—the mothers trying to soothe the babies and those offering unwanted advice on how to do so.

I don't know this place. I don't know shit. There's only Eury's trembling hand that I clutch in mine. We run downstairs to the church's basement. Remnants of last night's party are still intact with deflating balloons and a Happy Birthday sign taped to the wall.

I make sure the windows in the basement are closed.

"Who's out there that has got you like this?" I ask. "Tell me who and I'll go out and confront them. Who is he?"

The windows begin to shake. It must be the wind.

"He's trying to get in," she says, freaking out.

"Ain't nobody coming in here. And if they do, they have to come through me."

I puff my chest out. I've been in fights before. This isn't new. I can handle myself. If I have to throw down, I'm ready. The rattling continues. We can still hear the babies screeching upstairs.

"It's Ato. He's out there."

Eury points to the window. I grab a chair and press my face against the glass. There's no one there. Only the rain. What is it?

"He'll find a way in," she says. Eury cries. She can't stop trembling.

"Where? I don't see him." Whoever is messing with her is about to get beat. I sit Eury down. I'm going to find him. I'm not here for stalkers or fools trying to mess with my people. I'mma let him know. I may not be from the Bronx, but I gets down like I am.

"I'mma take a good look around. Make sure whoever is out there trying to scare you is going to stop, because I'm going to make him stop."

"Don't go out there. Please."

I kneel in front of her.

"Just gonna poke my head out. That's all. I'll be right back. No one is going to come in here. No one."

There is a stick used to open the large stained-glass windows. It's not a bat, but it will do.

I head back up the stairs and do a slow creep around the corner to where Eury said this guy Ato was standing. I hold tight to the stick, ready to wield it across Ato or whoever is causing Eury such harm.

I turn the corner and for a split second, I see a figure. The slender body of a boy crouched down, peeking into the basement window. It's got to be him. I make a run for it.

But when my footsteps get closer, there is no one there. I could have sworn I saw a person. He probably ran as soon as he heard me stomping toward him.

The blocks surrounding the church are equally deserted. Not a soul around except for some churchgoers lingering in front. This Ato guy must be quick to be able to bounce without a trace. Damn. This stalker followed Eury to the park, and now he's trying to show up at church. I'm not having that.

"Stop messing with Eury or I'm going to end you!"

I yell this at the top of my lungs. Let them all know what's up. Whoever is doing this is not going to get away with it. Not while I'm around. He's going to know what's what.

"Yo, shut the fuck up!"

A guy from the apartment building across the way responds the only way people from the BX do, by cursing me out. I know he ain't the one, so I let it go and return to the basement. Inside, Father Vincent has once again taken control of the mass. Babies are no longer having a fit.

Eury sits where I left her. Although her hair shields her face, I can still follow her tears streaming. I feel all kinds of bad. I kneel down in front of her.

"He's gone."

"Did you see him?" she asks with urgency. "Did you see Ato?"

She knows this dude. A guy she used to roll with, huh? His name is Ato. What kind of name is that? Ato is the type of nickname a guy gives himself to sound cryptic and cool.

"I thought I saw him. A guy crouched down looking through that window." I point to the same spot she was glued to earlier. "When I reached him, he was gone. I don't know where he booked it to. It was still raining."

"Did you really see him?"

She clutches my arm. This is important. There is this fire in her eyes. She needs this validation. I wish I had grabbed the guy. Given him the four knuckles. No one should be afraid to walk the streets. No one should have to live a life in fear because of some dude.

"What did he do to you? He was at the park, wasn't he?" I shake my head. I don't like this. My anger rises up. I feel like breaking something fragile, hearing a bottle shatter into pieces. She hesitates. I don't want to push her into reliving trauma. But who am I kidding, as if she's not reliving it right now.

"I'm sorry you are going through this. What can I do to help?"

The sun pierces through the window, shining a light on her. I brave it and place my palm over hers. I don't want Eury to be scared. Whoever is doing this to her must know they are also doing this to me. We stay like this for a long minute, until her hands stop shaking.

"You good leaving?"

Eury nods. We walk up the stairs alongside each other. The mass has reached the part where they are giving out the body and blood of Christ. I wait to see if Eury wants in on this. She stops before the exit, squeezing my hand. I squeeze back. I'm here for her. Whatever she wants or needs. I'm here for Eury.

She closes her eyes tight, mouthing the words to a prayer. I pay real close attention to who is around us. A guy walks his pit bull. A family is ready to enter the church for the next mass. Every single person is a suspect in my book.

"The D. Pater Company has given me their word that the church will not be put up for sale." Father Vincent has moved on to community announcements. "The new buildings will be multi-use. This will be a great time to welcome new parishioners into our flock."

"I'm ready," Eury says.

We step out to the front of the church. There are no clouds in the sky. It's hard to believe just minutes ago there was a downpour. I feel myself checking corners for this shadow of a guy.

"I want to tell you about Ato," Eury says.

I nod to her. This is a good thing. I need to get information on this boy Ato so I can start sending out my feelers. Everyone knows everyone on this block. If homeboy is making moves around Eury, I can easily find out.

"Okay. My father isn't home. We can talk there," I say. "I'm on the up-and-up. Te lo juro. You can trust me."

Eury accepts my invitation. She walks to the building, not really saying anything. We go extra quiet when we pass her aunt's apartment. My heart races a bit. I will get the biggest beatdown from Penelope's father if he thinks I'm up to no good with Eury.

My guitar rests against the wall where I usually leave it. I tap the wood for good luck as if I'm letting the guitar know I'm home. I also tap the ceramic elephant after placing the keys down beside it. I pick up my clothes spread all over the place in my rush to meet her this morning.

"Sorry." I shove them into my duffel bag. Why can't I be just a little bit more on top of things in my life? I can hear my mother's voice in my head telling me that a mess is a sure sign of disorder and mayhem. She never allows my room to be in disarray. How will Eury trust me if I can't even manage to put away my clothes or get to her on time? I got to do better. When I finish clearing up the mess and converting the bed back into a sofa, I urge Eury to sit down.

"You want tea? I can make us some. Chamomile. It's supposed to be good." I put the water to boil, and like a doofus, I wait for it. Man, I have no game in front of Eury. The player moves I've done before with other girls fall out the window. I don't know where to even place my hands. I grab a couple of mugs, then fill them with hot water and the tea bags. I sit down and wait for her to begin.

"Ato has been a part of my life for so long, ever since I was little." Eury takes her time. With every pause she looks up to make sure I'm following. "He appeared out of nowhere, right after my father left us."

"He came to the Bronx to torment you. That's messed up."

A long pause again. I need to shut up. I need to listen and keep my comments to myself because this is hard for her.

"Ato was my friend for a long time. He helped me, but

this changed as I got older, and I realized he wanted more from me."

Of course, sex. Homeboy tried to play that and it didn't go his way. Jerk.

"He wants to take me away from here. He keeps saying we belong together. The hurricane was his first act."

I shake my head. The hurricane? Ato did that? Eury is losing me. I don't understand.

"What do you mean the hurricane? How? Who is he?"

She's afraid to continue. The mug stays on the coffee table. Steam rises from the hot tea.

"Ato is Death," she says.

CHAPTER 12

Eury

He saw Ato. He saw him. Finally, Ato is no longer a secret I harbor alone. He is real and Pheus is my witness. This has to be enough. These scenes are not manifestations of stress like Mami says. It proves I am not making this up. I cling to this sliver of hope although Pheus nervously bounces his legs. His whole body generates anxiety. So does mine.

I'm at a crossroads here, the same turning point I faced earlier with Penelope. Do I continue to lie or do I allow Pheus a glimpse into this trauma? Penelope was unable to meet me halfway, but maybe Pheus will prove different.

He must. I have to continue.

"Ato isn't human. He's something unsettled. A spirit." I sound unsure. If I turn to Pheus, I will see how he doesn't believe me. He will give me the look Titi, Mami, and

Penelope have given me, so I don't. I stare at the mug in front of me and go on.

"Ato's not from this plane. He wants me to leave this place and be with him forever." My voice trembles because this is the first time I am actually admitting this to another person, the horror of Ato's unrelenting hunt to take me from this world.

"A spirit. You're talking about ghosts and shit?" Pheus says. He gets up. He sits down again. "Damn. Damn. But I saw him. I mean, I think I did."

He finds doubt, and because of that, I must try harder to change Pheus's mind. I keep talking, although this is way more painful than I could have ever imagined. Pheus can't turn away from the truth now, not when he stands so close.

"Ato wants me to live with him in el Inframundo. That's what he calls it. His home. Inframundo," I say. "He thinks I will be safe there. He destroyed Puerto Rico because I refused to go with him. Hurricane Irma was just a preview. Hurricane María showed what he was truly capable of doing. He followed me from Puerto Rico to Tampa, and now he's found me here. I don't know how to stop him."

Pheus shakes his head. But Ato did cause the hurricane. It was barely a year ago. I was there, and I will never forget it.

Our neighbors help us secure the house again. Mami gives them a gallon of water before they leave.

"Llámanos si necesitan algo," Blanca says.

"¡No va pasar nada! Va ser como Irma," Mami says before kissing Blanca 'bye. I'm glad Mami is so confident. I find myself checking the tarps on the window once more while she works in the front of the house. I go over our food and water supplies in my head. I think about the candles and the lighters we placed in ziplock bags.

"You don't have to bother." I jump at the sound of Ato's melodious voice. It's been almost three weeks since I last saw him, and in those weeks, I felt peace. I guess I just really believed he was gone, that my prayers were answered.

"Did you like it?" he asks.

"The jewelry box?" The gift is still hidden underneath my clothes. "Sure."

He laughs, and it sounds so jarring. "I mean the hurricane."

I stop what I'm doing. "What do you mean?" My heart races.

"I knew you didn't like the gift. I thought I might do something more to get your attention." He paces in front of me like a tiger ready to pounce.

"You are lying," I say.

"A little wind and rain to remind you how fragile life is here," he says. "In el Inframundo—"

"Stop this!" I am done with his threats that are masked in supplications. "Why would you think I would leave with you? I don't love you."

Over the years I've explained away his irrational behavior. Made excuses for his hostility toward anyone who befriended me.

131

I've tried to be patient. It was never enough for Ato. It's over. He must see what we had no longer exists, only in his warped mind.

"I will build you a home exactly the way you want it to be," he says. "You won't lack anything."

"You need to leave and don't ever come back." Although I'm trembling I must stand my ground. Ato can't have his way.

He faces me, and I know what will happen next. I have seen how his anger transforms him into a sinister beast. He is turning, and there is nothing I can do but watch in horror.

"I'll make you understand," Ato says. The sky loses its beautiful azure color. In its place the clouds roll deep and loom large. "You are meant to be with me. The sooner you see this, the easier it will be for you. Until then, you leave me no choice."

Ato's eyes turn completely black. The eyes of a demon. He loses his smile, his nose. His face becomes a blur.

"I will destroy what you call a home, and you'll realize this place is held up by the weakest foundation."

Oh my god. I run to the front of the house to find Mami.

"We have to take cover," I say, but Mami doesn't understand. She thinks I'm talking about Hurricane María.

"Eury, what's going on?" she asks.

I look out the window, and Ato stands there. First, he starts with the wind. The rains soon follow. He gestures, and a palm tree goes down. Then another. His face is unrecognizable. A flick from his wrist and a gust of wind shatters the living room window as if the tarps were made of tissue.

"¡Ay, Dios mío!" Mami screams. I grab her and run to the bathroom.

Ato continues the onslaught. Hours go by with Mami and me cowering in the bathtub. Crying and screaming with every jolt.

The walls on the house make an unnatural sound as if moaning. I look up toward the ceiling. Bits and pieces of the stucco start to fall down upon us. The ceiling itself shifts, jostled back and forth by Ato. Another groan from the foundation and I cling tighter to Mami. I am certain we are about to die.

"You are telling me this guy, this spirit, created the hurricanes that drove you out of the island? Is that what you are saying? How?" He slaps his hands together. "This is X-Men stuff, Storm levels. A being controlling the weather. Straight from the movies, yo."

He is trying to make sense of something indescribable. I'm losing him. Proof doesn't matter. I feel as if I am once again falling down a dark abyss.

"I don't know anything about this stuff," Pheus says. "Otherworld stuff. Evil ghosts. For real. I only know what's in front of me."

My heart slowly breaks. Pheus owes me nothing. Still, I try even when his denial fills me with a deep and utter hopelessness. Pheus said he saw him. Why can't that be enough?

"Pheus. You told me yourself, you saw a boy with curly hair. You saw him rattle the windows. You heard the babies screaming out like an alarm, alerting us. Ato was there, and then a second later he vanished," I say. "I'm asking you to believe me. Believe *me*. Please."

I can't stop the tears from falling. I'm begging him. Pheus, a boy I barely know, to truly see me. I didn't make this whole thing up. Our connection is real. The moment in the stairwell happened. The time he sang to me on the beach. Something unexplainable connects me to Pheus and Pheus to me. He can't allow fear to sever this tie. Pheus can't abandon me, not now.

He gets up again. He's scared. I'm losing him because of it. I get up, too, and face him. I seek any kind of bridge. I search deep in his eyes, and for a long moment we stare at each other. My heart pounds loudly. He must hear it. Feel it.

Pheus, believe me. Please.

But soon he averts his eyes.

I was wrong. I thought I was enough to change his mind. I'm proven once again to be utterly alone. But this embarrassment will not bury me into a sense of complacency. I can't afford that. I will stop Ato. If Pheus and Penelope are unable to join me in this battle, so be it. I rub away the tears. Disappointment will only weaken me. I let anger fuel me forward instead of despair.

I turn to leave.

"Wait a minute," Pheus says. "Where are you going?"

I don't answer him. I wish I could take back what I said, all of it. Pheus and his stupid songs. His saccharine declarations meant to charm. Worthless in the face of horror.

"Eury, you got to understand. This is new to me. I am trying to figure this out. To process it." He pleads for me not to leave. "What you are telling me is . . . wild."

Pheus stops himself from using the word "crazy." Of course. The word follows me like a scarlet letter.

"I'll give you as much time as you need," I say.

He is reluctant to let me pass, but eventually he does.

My family sees only a broken girl and now Pheus will see this as well. I don't slam the door behind me. To do so would be too much of a cliché. Instead, I close it softly.

⌒

"How was mass?"

I try my best to not let Titi Sylvia see my red face. My long hair aids in concealing me.

"Fine," I say and quickly walk to the bathroom.

People will eventually fail you. This is inevitable. This was true with my father, with Ato, and now with Pheus. Even with the allure of notes played on his guitar, Pheus floundered.

Why did I trust him? I fell for Pheus like every dumb girl in this neighborhood must have fallen countless times before.

"Eury, are you okay?"

My aunt softly raps on the bathroom door. I have to present myself. She can't see me upset.

"My stomach hurts. I must be getting my period."

"Oh," she says. "There's Motrin in the medicine cabinet. Take two. You want me to make you soup?"

"No, Titi. I should be okay."

I splash more cold water. I can't get Pheus's look of pity out of my head. He saw Ato. He did! For someone who says he believes only what's in front of him, surely that was more than enough proof. For the first time ever I had an anchor, a token connecting me to another. Ato wasn't all in my head—he was real, and Pheus saw him. Despite that, Pheus rejected me because he wanted a logical explanation that doesn't exist.

Relationships are finite. Every single one of them. It's what I've learned. I have to safeguard my heart. Protect this body from those who want to harm it. Even Pheus.

CHAPTER 13

Pheus

Let's be real. Eury is asking too much. She's talking about spirits. What the hell do I know about that stuff? Nothing. Nada.

And yet.

And yet, I saw what I saw. I heard the door and windows shake as if something was trying to get into the basement. I saw the boy. I saw him with my own eyes. This trigueñito dude. He looked a little out of place. He gave the impression of someone who had just arrived from the island. A little green. His halo of curly hair and the clothes he had on seemed out of date. I saw him long enough to get a sense homeboy wasn't from the neighborhood; long enough to get the feeling he wasn't down. The anger I felt was real. I was about to bash his head in. Rough him up and get to the bottom of why he's terrorizing Eury. There was no plan really. I was making decisions straight from the gut.

A quick turn of my head and he was gone. Nowhere to be found. I've seen shorties book. We each have innate skills when it comes to living in the city. Pops taught me how to enter a room, place your back to the wall, and count the exits. This boy could have the same type of skills. Someone who can blend in and out, cause Eury to second-guess herself.

Eury said his name was Ato. She knew him from Puerto Rico. A spirit.

This can't be happening. I don't know anything about anything about spectral stuff. Moms didn't bring me up that way. She raised me to see the world as it is: I have to work harder than everyone else. Strangers will build a false narrative based solely on hearing my last name or seeing me. Real, tangible obstacles meant to keep me down. Ato is a spirit. How do I respond to that? There are no such things as ghosts.

I'm taken right back to North Carolina when we were visiting Grandma Lynn, way before she became ill. The memory hits me raw.

One Thanksgiving, when I was ten years old, we visited Moms's family. I spent most of my time with my cousins Jay and Rudy. Jay was my age, his sister a year older. Thanksgiving in their home meant a different type of freedom. BBQs and green grass. Their upbringing was so different from mine.

Nature was always just outside their door. Even then, I knew what envy felt like.

That year Jay and Rudy were going on about how the tree outside their house was haunted. "Bad things happened there," they said. Jay told me to never climb the branches. If I stared too long, I could see them staring back. He didn't say who "they" were.

One night the cousins and I decided to explore. We armed ourselves with flashlights. I was determined to find out more about the tree. What were they talking about? As their stories became more and more sensational, my curiosity intensified. Why did they get strange beings living in trees? There was nothing like that in the city. What made Rudy and Jay so special? Even back then I thought they were a little dumb. Jay was held back a year. Rudy was smarter, but she was a girl, and so I thought she probably didn't know any better.

"Go on." Rudy kept pushing me toward the big oak tree, daring me. In the darkness the leaves on the tree made ominous shadows. Even the night noises seemed heightened.

"I'm not scared," I said.

My father's from the Bronx. What could a tree hold on my long lineage of resistance? Nothing, I thought.

When I stood under the branches and took the slowest look up, coldness covered my back, and I had trouble breathing. I squinted. Really tried to see. Something was staring down at me. Two glowing eyes, fluorescent red. Glaring.

I ran. Let my scrawny legs drag me as far away as possible from those devil eyes.

Behind me, my cousins cracked up. They rolled on the floor, hiccupping and punching each other. They called me country. I was the backward one, not my cousins.

"I thought people from the city were smart," they said.

Back then I swore I saw something up in that tree. The eyes haunted me for days until Moms reprimanded my cousins for putting notions in my head.

"Stop this foolishness," she said. And that was that. My cousins and I went on playing, but I avoided the tree the whole time.

Eury wants me to look up into them branches again. I can't. I'm scared, straight up. I don't have it in me, so it's easier to dismiss her.

Damn. I'm some real-ass punk. But it's my father's voice that's telling me to be safe, don't be stupid. Isn't that what I'm doing?

The sound of the doorknob turning trips me out. I jolt up and grab my guitar, ready to strike whatever comes through the door.

"What the hell?" Pops yells. "What kind of games you playing?"

He's pissed, tired from working and now having to deal with his paranoid son.

"Jesus. I can't come to my own place without getting accosted." Pops stomps to the bathroom and turns the shower on.

What kind of man am I if I can't even face the opening of a door? I ain't shit. Eury deserves better than my weak self. Music—including performing like a programmed robot onstage—is what I can offer. Not much else.

"What's wrong with you?" Pops still sounds annoyed, even after the shower. He opens the refrigerator, grabs butter and the carton of eggs.

"Nothing."

I can tell Pops anything, but I can't formulate what Eury told me. The stuff that happened at church. I'm still processing it in my head. I wouldn't know where to begin even if I tried.

He lifts the mug Eury held on to earlier but never took a sip from.

"You entertaining people here?"

Pops usually doesn't mind having Jaysen or the other guys in the apartment. As for girls, there's an unspoken rule: I'm not allowed to bring them here. Mom doesn't want it and neither does Pops. I've never once broken this rule. Not with Melaina, not with anyone, except Eury. It didn't cross my mind how I was disrespecting my father's apartment. Eury needed solace and the apartment offered that. Well, it did until the moment she asked for true help and I bailed.

"Eury was here, she's Penelope's cousin."

"You know how I feel about that." The butter sizzles on the pan.

"She needed help." My voice raises way too many levels. I'm angrier over my own crap than breaking Pops's rule, but I am still foolish enough to try it with him.

"First, you are swinging a guitar to my face. Second, you bring a girl here when you are not allowed to have friends over without me knowing." He smashes the egg hard. Anger is simmering inside him too. Pops turns the heat down on the pan.

"Living here for the summer means you abide by the rules. If you are not feeling them for some reason, we talk it out," he says. "But the options are plain. You abide by them or we got a problem."

"I got a problem."

Pops gives me a hard stare. He thinks this is about having a girl over. It's not. I am struggling, and I don't know who to turn to or what to do.

"It's not that. I mean. Forget it," I say, defeated. "I'm sorry. I'll never bring a person here unless you know about it."

I go to the sofa. It's at this moment that I wish I had my very own room instead of the living room. There is no door for me to close and block out everyone. I want to hide the shame I'm feeling as I go over how I treated Eury when she asked for help. Deep guilt for not being strong. Denying her straight to her face.

The spoon slams down on the plate. Pops is the only man I know who likes to eat his food with a spoon. He says he can get more bang for the buck, scoop food up like a shovel. I grew up thinking this is how men eat until Mom's boyfriend pointed out my errors when he took me to a fancy Italian restaurant in Brooklyn. He made a joke. It never once bothered Mom how I used to eat with a spoon just like my father. The way Mom laughed along with her boyfriend, I knew I was wrong. I *was* country. Somewhere my cousins were still laughing at me.

It takes a while for Pops to talk to me, but I knew he would. Pops is not the type of person to stay angry.

"Let's start over, son." The strong aroma of ginger fills the air. He grates his own into a tea. When I have an upset stomach, he makes me drink a cup. The smell of ginger is the smell of healing.

"Sorry I violated your trust," I say.

"I accept your apology. What else is weighing on you?"

I'm not sure how to answer him. I would have to admit how I failed Eury, how I will probably continue to flounder. And does it really matter? I'm probably dead to Eury now. She will never talk to me, and I don't blame her.

"A friend asked me to believe in something outside of my scope," I say. "I don't know."

Pops lets the heat of the mug warm his fingers. It doesn't matter if it's summer and a hundred degrees, Pops will forever sip tea.

"Eury?"

"Yeah. She's going through things. I thought I could help her, but now I'm not sure I can."

"What makes you so certain? Why are you saying no before you even try?"

Because she's talking about ghosts. Because I'm afraid. But I don't say these things.

"What if I don't know how? What if she's asking me to believe in things not based on logic?"

He shakes his head. Pops is so disappointed.

"I never thought I raised you to quit before even beginning," he says. "This world is filled with things outside of what is deemed reality. The horrors we are meant to take in every single day. Microaggressions. Blatant aggressions. Violence. Surviving the streets every day is a miracle. How does logic play into the everyday terrors we are meant to overcome?"

He talks slow, draws out each word as if he's living every moment he's had to deal with bullshit. The burden weighs.

"Find compassion. If your friend is in need and you can help, then you are meant to do so," he says. "I'm not saying put your life in danger, but act with intelligence. You're the historian. Books are your weapons. Use them. Arm yourself with knowledge."

He's right. I dismissed Eury before even trying to do some research. I could have asked her questions, tried to get into the history of what's been going on. Created a timeline. All those things. Instead I built up a wall made of fear.

"She probably won't have anything to do with me now, not after how I reacted."

Pops gets up and pats my shoulder.

"Then you know what you have to do next. Don't you? Mend your ways."

The work is before me. Pops takes his mug and heads toward his room.

"I raised you to be a fighter. To be smart. Don't fall into doubt now. It's not part of your DNA," he says before entering his bedroom.

I grab my phone and send Eury a text. An apology. The phone rings, and I swear it's her.

"Yo, they changed things up. The Dīs-traction owners want to move the concert up. We are slotted for this Friday instead," Jaysen says on the other end. "Only five days to get ready."

Jaysen rambles on and on about the club. Singing at a nightclub is the last thing I want to do. Eury doesn't respond to my text. How do I make this right?

"Bro, are you listening to me? We got to impress the owner."

"Yes. This Friday," I say. "Gotta go. Check in later."

I hit Eury with another text. I know she read it. Nothing. It's early. I head downstairs and knock on Penelope's door with the hope Eury answers it.

"Yes?"

Penelope's mom eyes me through the door's peephole.

"Hi. I'm Pheus. I live upstairs. Is Eury around?"

"What do you want with her?" She is not going to open this door.

"I just want to speak to her for a second."

I can hear her step away. Imagine her walking over to Eury. There is mumbling I can't make out. If only Penelope had answered the door. I would have bypassed her mother or at the very least got a message to Eury.

The door unexpectedly opens. Penelope's mom glares back at me with a distrusting face.

"Eury's not feeling well. She does not want to talk to you."

She slams the door shut before I can respond. It's definitely going down like that. No way around it. I got to take action and make this right. Eury reached out to me and I slapped her hand away. Now I have to rectify this situation.

CHAPTER 14

Eury

Penelope smells like the ocean. The familiar scent permeates the bedroom, and thoughts of home overwhelm me. It doesn't matter how long I've been away or what new city I land in, the island is never far from my thoughts. A scent, a familiar phrase uttered by someone, a song. Signs are presented to me on a daily or sometimes hourly basis, beckoning me back.

My cousin throws herself on the bed. Seconds later she grabs my shoulders and forces me to join. I allow myself to topple with her. I close my eyes and settle into pangs of homesickness mixed with the painful betrayal I'm trying to conceal.

"Aaron is so sweet," Penelope says. "He gave me this."

She shows me a heart-shaped gold necklace, the type of jewelry we would have wished for back when we were younger.

I try my best to seem interested, to continue to pretend that everything between us is fine.

"I know. It's not like we are in junior high. It's mad corny. Still I think it's cute," she says. "Aaron's definitely going to get some."

Penelope places her head against mine. We stay like this for a while, a position we would hold for hours when she would come visit me.

"Prima, Mami mentioned Pheus came by asking for you." She's eager for Pheus and me to be something. Perhaps she thinks Pheus can save me, a distraction to lift me out of this darkness.

"Yes, he did," I say. I move my head away from her. She notices.

"You don't like Pheus like that?"

There's a long pause. Pheus and my family think I'm losing it, and maybe I am. It's impossible to explain what is unexplainable. Each time I open my heart and tell the truth, I am crushed. I can't do it anymore. I will seal myself off from feeling anything. Lock myself up in my aunt's apartment until the summer is over. These walls will keep me safe from Ato. For now.

"No. I don't like him like that."

Penelope sits up straight and stares at me. She waits for me to break from what I said. Penelope wasn't there when Pheus doubted my story. Pheus heard the windows shaking.

He was just as scared as I was. We witnessed it together, and yet it wasn't enough.

My phone buzzes again, and I know it is Pheus leaving me another message. I've ignored every one of them. Seconds later, Penelope's phone goes off. Pheus is trying to contact me. Penelope glances at her phone.

"What is going on between you two?" she asks. "Did you see him today? Was this the reason why you didn't want to go the beach? If you wanted to see him, I wouldn't have stopped you. You're not telling me what's going on. Why aren't you letting me in?"

This isn't simple. I'm angry at her for telling her mother and at Pheus for proving he's a coward. As for me, I'm mad at exhibiting any vulnerability to them. The longer we sit in silence, the more my resentment grows. How could she turn on me when I asked for help? I can't contain this any longer.

"Why did you tell Titi?" I ask. "After I begged you not to, you told her anyway."

There's a slight recognition. Penelope can't deny it. She broke her promise.

"I was scared. I still am. I want to help you, but I don't know how," she says with such defiance, as if betrayal was her only option. She won't apologize for what she did.

"And you wonder why I'm not telling you anything important? I can't trust you," I say. "When we were kids, you didn't even blink when I told you a little boy talked to me. You said,

'Okay, what does he look like?' And I described every little detail about him. Do you remember what you said after? You said, 'I believe you.' Time changes everything, I guess."

I get up, locate the remote, and turn the volume on the television up. There's nothing else to say. Let the Weather Channel keep me company instead of this disappointment.

Penelope stands in front of the television screen. Her arms are on her waist. She will not move. Nothing hurts Penelope more than being ignored. She's not used to it. It's worse than a slap. I look down and let my hair cascade over my cheeks.

"Prima," she implores. I don't look up. This hurts. I want her to feel what I feel.

"Prima!" she yells. Her voice cracks. It's hard for me to sustain this. There's nothing valiant about going through pain alone. I only want one person to understand. Maybe not even to understand but just be there for me. Her running to Titi proved once again this anguish is to be endured alone.

"Don't do this. We're family. Don't shut me out." She doesn't hide her emotions. I can't keep this up because I'm not heartless, no matter how angry I am. I know she comes from a place of love. Penelope's afraid for me.

"Please, prima," she cries.

I finally look up. My tears flow too, even though I don't want them to.

"I don't have the tools to help you, so I went to Mami.

I won't apologize for that," she says. "We just want you to be safe. We love you, Eury."

I want to stay mad, to keep the rage burning, but I can't. I get up and hug her. We cry into each other's shoulders.

"I know you love me. I do," I say. "But what is happening with me can't easily be solved by talking to a doctor."

"How do you know?" Penelope says. "Your mother will only let you speak to priests."

"This isn't just anxiety from within," I say. "It's more than that."

"You say you are seeing a boy, but no one else can see him," she says. "What if it's a jumbling inside your mind? What if it's stress? Didn't this start right after Hurricane María?"

Penelope's scared the visions I'm seeing are only getting worse, that I don't have a strong hold on what is real or not. The episodes with Ato happened, and I can't simply capture them with my phone's video camera. Ato is coming for me. It's only a matter of time. This is my truth. I can't keep saying the same things over and over. I can't.

My head hurts. I sweat and start to shake. I don't know where to look or turn to. Penelope keeps asking me to explain, but I can't, and I'm failing. A black hole opens beside me, and I'm right at the edge of it.

"Eury, please. I'm trying to understand. Help me . . ."

It's getting harder for me to breathe. The walls in the room seem to pitch in toward me. I can't breathe. I can't. I bury my face in my hands.

"I don't know. I don't know. I don't know. I don't know . . ." I can't stop saying those three words. The abyss I'm falling down is endless. I can't stop. Penelope wraps her arms around me. "I don't know. I don't know . . ."

"Shhh. It's okay, Eury. Shhhh. You're not alone. I'm here. Your cousin is right here. I'm sorry. I'm so sorry." She rocks me like Mami used to do when I was young. We stay like this until my breathing returns and I am no longer spiraling.

"You can't talk about it right now. You don't have to. I'm so sorry I tried to make you," Penelope says. "I'm a horrible person. See, I don't even know what I'm doing."

"You are not a horrible person. How can I explain this?" I say. "Sometimes there are no solutions. Sometimes I don't know what I want or need. Right now I just want you to listen with an open mind. And if I'm too afraid to be alone, please stay by my side."

"I will promise to be here for you," she says. "But if I can't handle it, I have to find someone who can. That might be my parents, that might be another adult. It's not fair for you to expect less from me. Please don't ask me to."

I understand the terrible position I placed her in. The only way we can get through this is if I'm honest. Brutally honest. If that means she must talk to Titi afterward, I have to respect her wishes.

"I won't," I say. "I promise."

"There's something you need to know." She wrings her hands. This isn't going to be good. I brace myself for the news. "I heard Mami talking to your mom. Mami wants to take you to see a therapist friend of ours. Your mother had a fit. They really got into it over the phone. Your mother got so angry, she decided to pick you up earlier. She's coming next Monday."

Practically a week from today, Mami will scoop me up from the Bronx. I don't want to go back to Tampa. I need to hide. Go somewhere else.

"Going back to Florida won't make a difference," I say.

"So what do we do?"

We rack our brains for any type of solution, a sign that will show us there is a way out of this hell.

That's when I hear it. The strumming of a guitar floats from outside the window. Pheus sings a sorrowful bolero. The song is "Sombras Nada Más" by Javier Solís. A lamentation meant for me to hear.

"Apparently someone is in their feelings tonight," Penelope says. This finally breaks the tension, and we laugh.

The song continues. It stirs something deep within. What is it about Pheus and his music that confuses me? He hurt me. Yet, he tries to serenade the hurt away. It must be easy for him to do such things, to discard a girl's feelings simply with a verse.

I don't even realize when I'm standing by the window. I close my eyes and no longer see Pheus looking downcast nor do I see Ato's rage. What I see is my home the way it used to be. The smell of the papayas ready to be eaten. The sway of the palm trees. With each strum of Pheus's guitar, I am transported to a place where there is no anger or fear. Of course that doesn't exist, only when my head allows me to imagine it.

How can a song so sorrowful fill me with such a yearning for home?

The melody ends and Pheus starts another. This time the song is Agustín Lara's "Noche de Ronda." He continues and sings another. A soundtrack of grief and beauty blankets the summer sky.

"I lied," I say. "I do like him."

"Psss. Girl, I know you do."

I reach for my phone and read the many messages he left me. So many apologies. He wants to help. There are links to articles about spirits. Images from pages out of books from his home. Even a verse from the Bible.

Do not let your hearts be troubled. You believe in God, believe also in me. John 14:1

I chuckle at this. I'm not sure if he's taken the scripture out of context. It doesn't matter. The gesture is real.

Meet me in the hallway, I text.

"I'll be right back."

Without having to explain, Penelope joins her mother in the living room and stops her from following me to the door. She distracts her by showing Titi the necklace Aaron gave her.

I open the door just when Pheus arrives.

"Hi," he says.

I don't say anything. I stare at him and take in every feature. His full lips. His bushy eyebrows. The lines of his haircut. He is perfect and flawed, like me.

"I'm sorry," he says.

I take his hands and feel the hard skin on his fingertips, obtained from hours of playing the guitar.

"I'm sorry," he says again. He draws nearer. With his other hand, he tucks the long strands of my hair behind my ear. "I believe you, Eury. For real."

I exhale. I hadn't realized I was holding my breath.

"I believe you, Eury." Pheus says again. He presses his forehead against mine. Our fingers are now interlocked.

Pheus won't kiss me. He is too much of a gentleman. Instead I take the lead. I lean forward, tug on his shirt until we are both so close. His lips are soft. Sweet. The kiss doesn't last long, only enough to remind me how our time together is limited.

"Ato won't hurt you," he says. "Not if I can help it."

His words will erect a wall around me. Penelope is also committed to me. Maybe it's possible. Pheus kisses me again, and this time there is an urgency. Only a handful of days to avoid Ato. Then I leave the Bronx and return to more of the same.

At least I don't have to do this on my own. Penelope will stand by me. And Pheus? He believes me. He believes.

⟩⟨ PART II ⟩⟨

Arriv'd, he, tuning to his voice his strings, thus to the king and queen of shadows sings.

METAMORPHOSES BY OVID, TRANSLATED
BY SIR SAMUEL GARTH, JOHN DRYDEN, ET AL.

Tal vez me alimentaba el ego y fue mi error.
No sé en pocas palabras desubicación.

"TUYO," ROMEO SANTOS

CHAPTER 15

The suit I'm wearing is electric blue. There's a satin feel to the slacks and jacket. The T-shirt underneath is black with a slight V-neck. My chest hairs are making an appearance tonight. I'm going full-on Romeo and not holding back. Not one bit.

"Te botaste," Jaysen says when he checks out my threads. He insisted on wardrobe approval. I told him the last person who picked out my clothes was my mom, and that was when I was eight. Unless he birthed me, he needed to leave me alone.

We wait for an Uber to take us to the club. I hold my guitar case close. My nerves are shot. It doesn't help I haven't had much sleep. These past few days went way too fast. It's funny how cruel time can be. When you are at school, the clock just toys with you, its seconds slowly moving. In the summer, it's a joke how quickly time flies.

Every day I woke up eager to see Eury. She didn't want to go outside, and I was cool with that. The stairwell in my building became our second home. I would bring my guitar to practice while she borrowed Penelope's laptop. We sat next to each other on the steps. There were times when the neighbors would be annoyed by the noise. Other times when they would enjoy it. It would depend on the song I played.

When you don't have nearby parks, and it's too cold to be outside, the hallways have always been a great substitute. Jaysen and I used to play hide-and-seek in the building, finding shelter in one of the exits or janitor's rooms. With Eury beside me, sitting close, I felt like a kid again. We talked about everything. Her life on the island. My parents' divorce. School. Lack of school. Our fears.

And we kissed. Damn, we kissed. Every second, I wanted to touch her. I wanted the world to stop. Let us have our own space, outside of the ticking clock that has her mom taking her back to Tampa. With each kiss she would whisper my name like a sigh. Pheus. It didn't matter how hot it got inside that hallway or how many times her aunt gave me the icy glare; it was on.

My friends assumed I ghosted them because I'd been getting ready for the gig. Melaina sent me a long email with pictures of what she intended to wear tonight. I still haven't responded.

"Come through." Jaysen is on the phone wrangling more people to the show. He wears an insane-looking shirt with a dizzying pattern. If I didn't know better, I would think he was Dominican with his loud self. The Uber arrives and the driver has extreme merengue on. I ask him to lower the volume. He does so but only enough for me to hear Jaysen repeat a question.

"Did you get that?" he asks. "First impressions are important."

He tells me the owner's name, but I've already forgotten it. I can't stop thinking about Eury. How am I supposed to perform knowing she will leave for Florida in less than three days?

"Yo, concéntrate," Jaysen yells. "When you go inside, make sure you give the man in charge the hard handshake. Don't wuss out on this part. You've got to show up as a man, not a high school nobody."

Shake hands with the dude. Yeah, I got it. I know how to present myself no matter the circumstance. I've been code-switching since the first word came out of my mouth.

Pops said he's showing up tonight. He convinced his bike crew to join him. Mom can't make it. Her boyfriend planned a weekend getaway for them. She sent me money to celebrate afterward and made me promise to videotape it.

When the car stops at the front of the entrance, the crowd goes wild. Friday night, and there's a line of people waiting for the club to open. I search for Eury, but she's not here. I told her that her name would be on the list. She, Penelope, and Aaron are my special guests. I step out of the car, and people pull out their phones, filming me like I'm somebody. They came to see me. It's ridiculous, and I love every second of it.

Melaina's not waiting on this line. She's already behind the velvet rope with her girls. She walks over to me and plants a wet one on my cheek. Thalia is ready, taking pictures of us together. I smile at the camera, and I'm glad Eury is not around. For Melaina, this is a show.

"Good luck, baby," she says.

She tries for another kiss, but I pull back. Enough with this charade. Anger no doubt courses through her, but she won't display it. Although Melaina hasn't seen me with Eury, I'm sure she's heard about us.

Jaysen gives the bouncer the what's-up. I walk toward the thick wooden doors into the club.

Tonight I want everything to go as planned. We celebrate and enjoy ourselves. One last time before Eury leaves.

On my way, Eury texts.

Aaron promised to drive Eury and Penelope right to the club and drop them in front. I also made him swear to be on the lookout for Ato. No one is to press up on Eury. While

I'm onstage, Eury will go directly backstage and enjoy the show from there, far from the crowds. That's the plan.

The Kingsbridge Armory takes up a whole block. They really are trying to make the place dizzyingly ritzy. High-class entertainment with separate spaces for children and adults. The restaurant is located above the club while the indoor roof-top pool is encased in glass so everyone can enjoy the sky no matter the weather.

We enter the restaurant first. They've spared no expense. Everything is completely mirrored and gilded. I guess gold makes a person feel luxurious, and it also creates an abundance of light. There are tables upon tables with champagne bottles already on ice. Those occupying the tables are dressed Manhattan fly. Outfits definitely not meant for this neighborhood. And just like in a restaurant in New York, not one person pays us any attention. We are invisible.

"You belong downstairs," a bouncer, who looks identical to the one situated outside, says.

"Good looking out," Jaysen says.

The faceless bouncer slowly pulls back heavy velvet curtains to reveal a set of descending stairs. The scent of sulfur and incense permeates the staircase. I gesture to Jaysen to see if he smells it. He's too busy trying to be the man, walking down the stairs as if he knows where he's going. The heavy odor is not what I would normally expect from a nightclub.

The fragrance reminds me of St. Anselm and the various botánicas around the neighborhood. I feel as if I'm entering a holy place.

Instead of gold, the club below is a cavernous room draped in red. Red carpets. Red walls. A red bar. Even the stage has red floors. It reminds me of that old scary movie *The Shining*. I am not one to believe in bad vibes, that sounds way too corny, but this is a type of place Pops would declare un baja nota. There is no music being played, which adds to my uneasiness. I chalk up my apprehension to nerves.

The other musicians are already here. Their instruments are placed on the elevated stage, with a sizable dance floor situated right in front.

"Is Papo Sileno here?" Jaysen asks. He rubs his hands together. He's nervous too. Manager or not, this was his idea. Being so close to the decision-makers is what Jaysen always dreamed of. To run with the big rollers.

Almost there, Eury texts. I'll feel better when she's beside me.

Similar to the restaurant upstairs, there are tables strewn across the floor. The tables are small, only room enough for drinks. A beautiful, tall woman with a blank expression tends to the bar at the far end of the club. Two others soon join her. They look almost identical, as if the owners only employ a certain type. Like the bouncers upstairs, the workers ignore us. We are the help. No reason to acknowledge us.

I can't help but think to myself, *Just you wait. When you hear my voice, you will be unable to look the other way.*

"Jaysen!"

An older man with long, black hair has a hand firmly clasped on Jaysen's shoulder, while the other holds a glass of wine. His expensive shirt is unbuttoned, revealing a smooth chest. On his feet are cleft square boots that look like hooves. An outfit only someone with serious money would rock without fear of being ridiculed or beat down for being different.

"You must be el Nuevo Nene de la Bachata!" he exclaims. The man reeks of alcohol and he's got what I would call a horse face. "My name is Papo Sileno, but I go by Sileno."

I shake his hand hard, and he does the same. He also gives me the up-and-down. Sileno does not let go. Because this is a test, I stay firm. I will smile and be charming because Jaysen is breathing heavily next to me, praying Sileno likes what he sees.

Sileno lets go and runs his fingers against the lapel of my suit.

"Very smooth. He's perfect," he says. "Perfect."

Jaysen lets out a sigh of relief. He pats my back, hard. Why do I feel as if I've been sold?

"Have you seen the crowd?" Jaysen asks, eager to please. "They are ready."

"So am I," Sileno says. The glint in his eye reveals other

things. The woman behind the bar appears to refill his cup. He whispers to her.

"Let's toast."

I don't want to drink the red wine he offers from some unpronounceable place, but I do. I have to. I'm sealing the deal to play.

"Oh my god."

Penelope and Eury finally arrive. Penelope is dumbfounded by the ambience. As for Eury, she is scared, but when our eyes meet, her fear slowly dissipates. Eury is here. I don't care how Sileno is drinking another glass of wine, but I do care how he stares at Eury. Leers at her. When Eury stands beside me ready for introductions, I place my arm around her shoulders.

"This is my girlfriend, Eury."

"Bueno, Girlfriend Eury, you are a vision." Sileno kisses her cheek delicately, and I want to punch him in the face. Eury isn't feeling the spectacle. Still, she graciously smiles.

"Drink. Drink. This is going to be fun." He offers everyone wine. Eury takes only a small sip from the large goblet. "You might want to do a sound check. Don't worry, I will keep your friends entertained while you do."

I don't want to leave Eury alone with him. Sileno's a type of charming predator who probably thinks owning a club is enough to compensate for his questionable fashion sense.

"Go ahead," Jaysen says, giving me the eye. Jaysen should

be nervous. I'm about to pounce on this guy if he keeps licking his lips and staring at Eury like she's a sancocho.

I reluctantly join the musicians on the stage. Sileno continues to be boisterous and loud. Jaysen seems to love it. He probably wants to be like him, his apprentice in the art of bullshit.

Sileno tells Penelope a joke. Her laugh is an uncomfortable one. I strum my guitar hard. Aaron pays attention to the exchange and gives Sileno the hard stare. I need to get Eury away from him. I don't want her to continue to be nice to this jerk, not on my account.

"Hey, Eury, did you bring the thing I asked?" I say loudly into the microphone. My voice stops Sileno in midsentence of another dumb joke. His smile never leaves his face. Eury takes the hint and joins me onstage.

"I don't like that guy," I say.

"I can tell," she says. "He's pretty predictable. A grosero nightclub owner. It's a good thing I'm not into that."

The anger simmers down a bit. She is with me. We are going to be fine.

"I'm not here for that mama culo," I whisper. "Hang out backstage. Away from him."

She agrees to.

"Ready, el Nene?" Sileno yells out. "We are about to open the doors."

Although Sileno continues to drink glass of wine after

glass of wine, he doesn't appear drunk. He walks with an even pace. Sileno addresses his workers in whispers, but with us, he's obnoxious.

I wait on the side of the stage with Eury while people fill up the club. The music is pumping now. Couples take to the dance floor. I spot my father and his crew hanging back, letting the young people take up room. I see Penelope and Aaron dancing. Jaysen talks to important-looking men. Melaina has commandeered a table front and center.

"Don't be nervous," Eury says. "You're going to be great."

This is a mistake. What am I doing? Eury leaves on Monday, and we are wasting time in this cursed building with this elitist clown who is, right now, serving wine to Melaina.

"Let's go," I say. "I changed my mind. I don't want to do this."

Eury grabs the loop of my belt and draws me close.

"Sing as if you are only singing to me," she says. "I'll be right here watching. Three songs. Only three songs. For me."

We kiss, and it's the courage I need. I can do this.

Sileno takes to the stage. He gives me a nod. We are about to begin.

"Welcome to Club Dīs-traction, the premier house in the Bronx for live music and libations. I'm the owner, Sileno, and I'm very proud to introduce our first Young People's Night," he says. "We are hoping for more events like this. What do you think?"

The crowd yells and applauds.

"Now, I've heard so much about this boy. Everyone seems to be talking about him, from Orchard Beach to Third Avenue. He's going to be big and you are going to remember tonight. You heard him here first. Let's give it up for el Nuevo Nene de la Bachata, Pheus!"

My father whistles a loud street whistle used to hail cops and to alert kids to get off the street. My friends holler. I hug Eury and give her too quick of a kiss. The guitar is tuned. My voice is primed. I'm ready.

CHAPTER 16

Eury

There are so many people here in the audience sending Pheus love. Yet even in this crowded club, there is only us. Pheus and Eury. I am meant to witness this very moment without fear of the future. There's no Ato here to steal this away from me. There's only Pheus, and he is mine.

The owner of the club, Sileno, suddenly appears backstage. He smells of red wine and something else. Desperation? No. I can't quite place it. I do my best to move a couple of inches away from him.

Pheus raises his hand to settle the crowd. It takes a while, but eventually they listen. He strums his guitar. With a quick nod from Pheus, the musicians join him and begin to play. The first song is a cover of a Romeo Santos tune, a popular bachata. Couples quickly take to the dance floor. Their bodies pressed so closely, so intimately. I'm reminded of my week with Pheus. Every morning I would wake with a text from him. I let him know I was eating breakfast. That I was dressing. We counted down the minutes until we could be together.

The hallway became our home. A safe place between our two apartments. My aunt was annoyed at how Pheus was always around but was unable to stop us from meeting at such an innocent landing.

The threat of Ato lingered on those steps; however, it didn't consume me. I was too busy laughing at Pheus's corny jokes. When we kissed good night, I felt the pressure of time slipping past us. Another day nudging me closer to a flight back to Florida.

"He's very good," Sileno says. He moves closer, and I step away. "Do you sing?"

"No."

"Aw, you must be a dancer," he says. "I can show you some moves. You can share them with your boyfriend later."

When Sileno says this, his fingers trace the side of my arm.

"Don't touch me," I say. It isn't hard to tell the type of man Sileno is. It was obvious the minute we were introduced. He looked at me and Penelope as if we were morsels to eat.

The crowd screams their love for Pheus, who finishes his cover. He looks my way, so filled with happiness. Next to me, Sileno continues to stare. A server replenishes his glass with more wine. She holds out another glass to me, and I decline the invitation.

"You don't drink?" he asks.

"I'm only seventeen," I say.

"I won't tell anyone."

Pheus is about to sing a new song, the one he's been working on all week. I hush Sileno. It doesn't stop him. He continues to ask me why I'm not drinking. A row of girls intensely stare at Pheus as if they want to consume him. Sileno has a similar expression. He flirts and buzzes near my ear.

"Cállate—" I say as Sileno clumsily spills wine on the blouse I borrowed from Penelope. The red drips down to the floor like a wound.

"Oh no, I'm so sorry," Sileno says.

"Just get away from me." I leave in search of a bathroom to clean myself up. I'm so angry. I don't want to miss the rest of the performance.

"Where's the bathroom?" The beautiful servers are so mesmerized by Pheus's voice they ignore me. I finally locate one up a flight of stairs. I enter the empty bathroom and lock the door. I stink like wine. There is no way I will be able to get rid of this stain. The more water I add, the more the color spreads. Idiot. I should have sat by Penelope a long time ago.

I can hear Pheus's melodic voice, stronger than I've ever heard him sing before. He calls to me from the stage. At first, he whispers my name. There's a long pause, and the crowd goes silent. Then Pheus sings my name aloud. The audience yells in approval. Although I'm not seeing him, if I close my eyes I can still follow his gestures. He will have his eyes closed too. We will think of each other.

There's only one more song left for Pheus to sing. I won't miss it. I'll find Penelope to avoid any further interruptions. If I hurry, I can still make it.

I open the door. Sileno is there.

CHAPTER 17

Pheus

I've sung this Romeo Santos song thousands of times, and yet tonight is different. This isn't like playing on the beach with my friends. Back there, it didn't matter if I flubbed a line or two. I never took it seriously. On this stage, I feel the surge of the energy from the audience. It feeds me. Got me feeling ten feet tall. With every verse, I can make couples dip closer to each other. When I hit the right note, the girls in front of the stage lean in. They watch my every move, and I ain't gonna lie, I like it. I got this audience right in my hand.

Although I can't turn to Eury every second, I can feel her presence. There is love. My first love. I'm not talking about lust, the desire to get with someone. This is more. The days we spent together this week sealed it for me. I haven't said the three words to her, but I have shown them with my actions.

I hope she can feel it. All them cheesy-ass romantic sayings hit me like a sledgehammer. Even if Eury has to go back to Tampa, we'll figure it out. Jaysen says que yo estoy borracho de amor like Beyoncé. He may be right. Estoy asfixia'o.

It's time to hit them with another song. This is the one I've been waiting to sing. My song for Eury. She's heard bits and pieces of it throughout the week. Tonight it makes its debut. A love song dedicated to her.

"This song goes out to the special person in your life. The one that can see you. The one that doesn't take shit from anyone. Tu amante," I say. "The song is called 'Mi Promesa.' 'My Promise.'"

Because these lyrics are so raw, I close my eyes.

"Eury."

My voice is almost at a whisper. It's just me and the guitar. I sing her name again, this time louder. These are the lyrics I've said to Eury this week. The promise to believe her. To strip away my doubts and listen.

The second verse I confess my love. This I have not shared with Eury. The girls in the audience swoon. The boys are making them love connections. When I open my eyes, Eury is gone. She must have decided to go with Penelope. I keep going.

The last song is a quick bachata, a number everyone can grind to. The only tune that will guarantee this is Joan Soriano's "María Elena." It's sexy and fun. I play it fast so the dancers can swing their partners at a dizzying speed. The musicians keep up with the pace.

I grab the mic and practically lean off the stage. The girls pull on my sleeves. They want me. I keep singing. Their adoration fuels me. This feeling is a hundred times more electric than singing to my friends. I crave more, laughing and giving everything I got to the audience.

"¡Otra! ¡Otra!"

They don't want me to stop. Jaysen signals for me to sing another. I turn to the band and tell them to play a classic bachata by Antony Santos. They know the one. Those in the audience sing along with me. There's nothing like this. The girls swing their hips. The boys holler. This crowd living for me is a high, and I can't get enough. The clapping seems never ending. I can sing for hours. My smile is ridiculous and large. Is this what Romeo Santos feels when he plays in those big stadium concerts? If it is, I want more.

"Bro, you did it!" Jaysen jumps on the stage and hugs me. Strangers grab my arm and pull me toward them. So many phones trying to capture this moment. It's straight-up chaos, and I can't stop laughing. It takes a while before it finally dawns on me. Eury is not around.

"Have you seen Eury?" I ask in between girls posing for selfies with me. Jaysen shakes his head. This doesn't feel right.

CHAPTER 18

Eury

Sileno blocks the exit. I know what he wants. The crowd continues to scream for Pheus. No one will hear me if *I* scream.

"Please let me help," he says.

"Leave me alone."

His leer turns into a scowl. I try to push my way through, but he is stronger than me. His boots look like the hooves of a horse. They clop against the tiled bathroom floor. Sileno presses his face against mine. I kick and cry out. He won't let me go. He tries to force his disgusting thin lips on mine. When I turn away, he thrusts his whole body forward.

There is a window above me, a small one. The window-pane begins to shake.

Ato is outside. He sees what Sileno is trying to do.

"Hey! Get out of there," Sileno yells. He notices the young boy with brown curls. Ato jolts the window even more. He's trying to break through.

"Hey! Away from the window."

I use the interruption to push Sileno and run out of the bathroom. Outside, Ato waits for me. I can't go out there. I go down the steps, toward the restaurant.

"Please, help me."

The woman is tall and offers only a dead expression. There is no compassion. She looks straight through me.

"Please!"

The server instead offers me a glass of wine. I look over to the crowded restaurant. Those seated raise their glasses at me in a toast. Every single one of them with the same empty expression. They are part of this deception. Monsters. They are like Sileno, and this is a trap.

"¡Otra! ¡Otra!" The audience yells for Pheus to sing another song. I'm stuck in this building with a beast trying to rape me and an evil spirit outside waiting to kill me.

Melaina enters the restaurant. I run to her. When she sees me, she is cold, then notices the growing stain on my blouse and grins.

"The owner won't leave me alone." I'm near tears, unable to control my trembling.

"So?" she asks.

"Please help me." I grab her arm. I can hear Sileno's voice.

He directs the servers to continue pouring wine to those things sitting at the tables. I need to get away. "I'm begging you!"

"Fine. Go to the roof. I'll tell Pheus and Penelope to look for you there," Melaina says. "Don't worry. I'll stop this fool. He won't find you. Go."

I hug Melaina because she is helping me even though she hates me. I'm covered in sweat as I run up the stairs. I pass the neon green sign that reads This Way to the Estigio Pool. The door leading to the rooftop pool isn't locked. I push it open.

The pool is enclosed in a glass atrium. It is dark, but the moon illuminates my way. The place is empty. I send Pheus and Penelope texts, alerting them to where I am. They do not respond. There is a bar at the far end of the pool. I crouch down and hide behind it and wait. There's nothing else to do but recite my prayers.

Please, Pheus, be quick. A prayer for Pheus to find me.

There is the sound of a button being pressed. The glass ceiling of the atrium slowly opens. I hold my breath. Sileno is here.

CHAPTER 19

Pheus

"Where is she? She was right by the stage." I corner Jaysen. I have an awful feeling. This is not good. I can feel it in my gut.

"I haven't seen her," Jaysen says. "There's somebody here who wants to meet you. A record producer."

The man is dressed in the latest in hip-hop fashion. He screams money.

"One second," I say before I'm pulled in from behind. It's Pops.

"Proud of you, son. You gave it your all. Enjoy this moment," he says. His friends congratulate me. This feels good, but it's missing Eury.

"Thanks, Pops. Have you seen Eury?"

The first time he met her, Pops gave her a book of poetry

by Neruda. Eury and I would take turns reading the verses aloud to each other. Pops said Eury has a good spirit and that I should do right by her. It wasn't a warning, just a reminder to keep those you love close.

"No. I thought I saw a glimpse of her offstage," he says. "Don't stay here too long. This building contains too much trauma."

Before I can get Pops to elaborate, another group of girls asks for a picture.

"I'll let you get on with it." Although he is smiling, I can tell Pops is feeling the uneasiness I'm feeling. "Be safe. Don't be stupid."

He walks back toward the bar. Pops won't stay long, not when the price of a drink is so steep. He'll continue to celebrate by the park.

I try my best to give people love, but honestly I just want to bounce. My phone has been turned off so as not to distract me or mess up any sound. I turn it back on. It's taking too long to start up.

Melaina slinks over to me.

"Have you seen Eury?" I sound like a broken record.

"Who?" she says. "I don't know her."

"Stop acting out of pocket." I look at my phone. It's still not working. "Did you see her or not?"

Melaina makes with the duck lips. She can't be this heartless. I ask again. Melaina huffs.

"She said something about someone bothering her. I told her to wait for you on the roof." Penelope takes a long sip from her drink. "Also, there was this guy outside asking about her. A boy with curls. Competition?"

Ato. My heart sinks.

"Don't say I never gave you anything," Melaina says with a laugh.

It's hard to navigate this crowd. No one wants to leave, and everyone wants a piece of me. Jaysen motions for me to meet the producer.

"I can't do this right now," I say. "I'll be back." His face is a wall of disappointment.

Eury is up on the roof. I don't know what's going on, but she's by herself. Nothing else matters until I see her. The dumb red color makes it difficult to find the right exit out of this cavernous room.

"How do I get to the roof?" I ask the statuesque server who looks like a robot. There ain't nothing real about her. Nothing.

"It's off-limits," she says with this deadness in her tone like she's reading from a script. "You are not allowed up there."

"The fuck I'm not."

"You heard her." A bouncer appears out of nowhere.

"Get out of my way."

He blocks the path to Eury. I don't know if Ato got to her or not. This bouncer will get out of my way, or I will tear this club down. If I have to take this table and bash it across his chest, I'll do it. My hands form a fist. This guy is twice my size. I'm still going to plow through him with everything I got. "I'm telling you right now, I'm going up."

Before I throw the first punch, Melaina shows up.

"A guy just pinched my ass," she says to the bouncer.

The bouncer doesn't react, but Melaina does.

"Are you going to just stand there? Do something or I'm going to take this bottle and cut his face."

Melaina points to a group of sloppy clubgoers. As if living up to the stereotype, one of the guys grabs another girl's ass. The girl turns and slaps him. He laughs. Within seconds, the bouncer barrels toward him and lifts him by the shoulders. Melaina tilts her head to the steps while the bouncer and the guy scuffle on the floor. I give her a nod and take to the stairs.

CHAPTER 20

Eury

Flashes of lightning streak across the sky. My heart pounds so loudly. Ato must be near.

Please, Pheus. Please come.

"It cost so much money to have this atrium built," Sileno says. "I told them I didn't care. I wanted this place to outdo the clubs in the city. You can see why it was important. I have many people to impress."

Sileno's hooves make an eerie *clip-clop* only horses should make. He walks toward the bar. I grab a half-empty bottle of wine. I'll break it over his head. He won't touch me. I'll kill him before he does.

"There you are," he says.

I stand, holding the bottle firmly.

"Get away from me."

Sileno's eyes are as red as the club where Pheus now sings an encore. Can't Pheus tell I need him? Can't he sense my desperation?

"What's this about?" Sileno says. "I only came here to make sure you were okay. My job is to assure my guests are well taken care of."

I move away from the bar. The stairs are just past the pool. Maybe I can get to the exit before Sileno reaches me. There's another flash of lightning. Ato wouldn't let Sileno hurt me. He wouldn't. So here I am hoping Ato will save me from Sileno. A choice between two devils.

Sileno lunges. I raise the bottle, but he doesn't stop. I hit him with everything I've got, right on the head. The bottle shatters into pieces. He slumps to the floor. There's wine and blood everywhere, but I have no time to waste. I must get to Pheus.

"Eury."

Ato floats down from the sky. His feet barely touch the deck. His eyes are not yet black coals. Ato radiates light as if he's being charged by the moon. I shake my head. This is not real. This is a nightmare I can't wake up from.

Sileno groans on the floor beside me.

"It's time, Eury," Ato says.

"No one is taking me," I say. "Not Sileno and not you."

The broken glass makes the floor slippery and slick. With each step I feel untethered, but I have to get to the stairs.

My phone goes off. It must be Pheus. I can't respond.

Por dios, Pheus, find me.

"Pheus will do the same to you," Ato says. "Don't you see how little he cares? The only thing he loves is fame."

I shake my head.

"Why, Ato? You once said you loved me. This isn't what love is," I say. "You are like Sileno here, a monster only wanting to own me like I'm some toy. Please let me go."

The steps I take are tiny, each one accompanied by a crunch. Glass embeds into my heels.

Pheus. Come quick.

"You won't have to worry about Sileno or your mother or the hurricanes anymore," Ato says. "There will be an abundance of time in el Inframundo. I promise."

With each word, his face mutates. He is the little boy I first met in front of my house. He changes again, and he is a bit older. The face of the boy who spent hours with me exploring the rivers. He shifts again and his eyes are black, the same face that appeared to me right before he directed a hurricane to rip the walls off my house.

I take another step closer to the door. I sense Pheus will be here soon. I just need a little more time.

"I belong here. I'm not meant to be with you, Ato. Can't you understand?"

"Do you remember when we first heard the song 'Adore'?"

The sound system plays the song on cue. Ato didn't even lift a finger to make this happen.

"We decided Prince was probably not of this world. Remember?" he says. "We built a shrine to celebrate him. I will do the same for you."

"You don't have a right," I say. "You are a parasite. Thousands died because of your jealousy. My home destroyed because of a fantasy you've created. There is no us. There never will be."

I hear a rush of footsteps. Pheus is coming. I move. Ato inches closer to me. I slip but get up as quickly as I can. I try my best to move lightly. If I make a run for it, I will surely fall and that will give Ato the break he needs to reach me. How will he do it? How will he escort me to el Inframundo? Will he kill me simply with a touch?

The door slams open.

Pheus. Mi amor. Mi vida. He's here.

"No," Ato says. "It's too late."

He's wrong. I am leaving this roof with Pheus. These devils will not get in my way.

"Eury!" Pheus yells.

If I run with force, I can reach Pheus. He is so close. Pheus will protect me from this hungry spirit. He sees Ato, truly sees him. There is no doubt. Pheus sees my tormentor, and in return, I taste freedom.

The glass scattered on the floor is my enemy. There is a blinding light coming from the sky. Another flash of lightning followed by rain. I can't see clearly. It's okay. Pheus is right there. If I go to him, I will be safe. Ato will be a distant dream, a nightmare. I will forever banish him from my life.

I make a run for it, but I can't hold my balance. I start to fall. The floor comes rushing toward me. A hard chrome edge lines the pool. It is shiny enough to catch my reflection, to mirror back my face of horror. Time slows down, a trick to show me how I will end. It is as slow as a heartbeat.

Pheus screams my name. My beautiful Pheus.

I can't stop this infinite fall. There's no way to brace myself. I will hit the side of this pool. What a way to end, with Pheus only an arm's length away, my chance of salvation closed off forever.

The edge of the pool rushes toward me.

"Pheus!" I scream.

CHAPTER 21

Pheus

The stairs are endless. My phone still hasn't turned on. I'm out of breath, but I keep going. The neon sign reads This Way to the Estigio Pool. I try pushing open the big black door, but it doesn't budge. I press my ear to the door. Voices sound muffled. I can barely make out Eury.

"I'm here, Eury!" I pound the door with my fists.

I can't tell if she hears me. I push against the frame using all my strength, but it only cracks open an inch. It's not enough. I make a running start, and the impact hurts my shoulders. I do it again. One more push.

"Eury! I'm right here!" I yell into the opening. Eury stands there, tears streaming down her cheeks. Her whole body shakes. She talks to someone. Is it Ato? I'm going to tear him apart.

"Get the fuck away from her," I shout.

One more push.

The door finally gives.

"Eury!"

I catch her tiny smile, a recognition of how I finally found her. A body lies slumped on the floor, and a few feet away is Ato. The boy I saw from the other day. He, too, has a smile, a sinister one. A strange glow emanates from him.

Ato looks over to me.

"It's too late," he says.

For a split second, his eyes become orbs of black. Eury was right. He is not from this world. I try not to lose it. How do I get to Eury? How can I protect her from this thing?

"I got you, Eury," I say. "He's not going to hurt you."

Lightning strikes. A blinding flash. Seconds pass slowly as we wait to hear the thunder that never materializes. Instead I hear a familiar song playing on the speakers.

Eury makes a break for it. She runs toward me. I'm waiting for her, my arms ready to take her away from this demon.

Her shoes are slippery. The floor is slick with something wet and red. She runs diagonally, but her feet fail her. She keeps losing her balance. I run to meet her halfway. I'm not going to catch her in time.

Eury falls, and I watch her head hit the side of the pool.

There is a loud *thunk*, and her whole body drops into the water.

"Goodbye, Pheus," the monster says.

No. Damn. No. No.

I jump into the pool and drag Eury out. A trail of blood trickles down and spreads across the water. Eury's eyes are closed.

"Eury, wake up. Wake the fuck up."

There is a gash across her forehead. Blood.

"Eury, I'm right here. Wake up."

She's not moving. Naw. Fuck this shit. Wake up. Wake up. Wake up.

I scream for help. This can't be happening. The song continues to play in the background, and I keep yelling for someone, anyone, to hear me. I check her heart. Her wrists. How is it I forget everything I've seen on those countless medical shows on TV?

Penelope and Aaron rush toward me.

"What happened?" Penelope asks. She grabs hold of my suit. Her nails dig deep into my chest. Aaron dials 911. The fire alarm has been pulled. More people are finding the roof. There is a circle of onlookers. Penelope keeps screaming. Aaron tries to calm her down.

Stop screaming, Penelope. This isn't over.

I use the sleeve of my shirt to dry Eury's face. The wail of an ambulance can be heard. They are coming. I lean over her.

"Please, Eury," I beg. "Wake up. Eury, I'm right here next to you. This is not how it ends for us. I won't let it end."

I kiss her cold cheek.

Eury, wake up.

Eury.

CHAPTER 22

Eury

Darkness.

CHAPTER 23

Pheus

Everything is wrong. People ask me questions, but I don't remember responding. Papo Sileno, the owner of the club, eventually wakes up. He said he blacked out and fell.

"I was drunk," Sileno says.

He's lying through his teeth. I store his lies in the back of my mind for later use. When he least expects it, I'm going to rain down on him because what happened to Eury most definitely is tied to him.

Eury is only a few feet away. She's surrounded by paramedics. The bouncers have pushed everyone to the side to give them space. Penelope is hysterical, crying on Aaron, who holds her tight.

The cops ask me questions, and I tell them what I know.

I don't tell them everything. The name Ato never escapes my mouth. I don't feel his presence. Ato is gone.

"What hospital?" I yell when the paramedics pull the gurney holding Eury. They respond with Lincoln. "Lincoln is too far. Take her to Lebanon."

"There's been a fire," the paramedic says. "Lincoln is our best bet right now."

"I'm going."

"We're not done yet."

A cop places his hand on my shoulder. He looks like every other cop out here. His partner is the good cop. She tries to be understanding, but it's an act. This is a play I've been dragged into to perform a part I never wanted. Eury is being taken away. Her face is covered with an oxygen mask. My crumbling heart is replaced with rage.

"We will text when we get there," Aaron says while keeping Penelope upright.

I sit down in a lounge chair. The cop continues to grill me. They ask me again and again what happened, and I repeat my version. I'm at fault here somehow. That may be true. I was too full of myself, soaking up the adoration of the audience instead of keeping Eury safe.

"I need to go," I say. The cops won't allow it.

"Just a few more questions," they say.

I check the time. It speeds so fast. An hour goes by, and

these cops continue to talk in circles. A half hour more, and I waste away while Eury is in Lincoln Hospital. Eury's going to be all right. She is. I won't accept any other reality.

"Where's my son?" Pops pushes through the crowd. He gets up in the cop's face. "He's a minor."

When I see him, I start to bawl like the day I found out my parents were getting a divorce. I can barely breathe. The emotions pour out.

"I tried to get to her, Pops, I swear." I can't stop crying.

"My son is done here," Pops says. "He's done."

The cop opens his mouth to say something but changes his mind. They let me go. I gather my stuff. Jaysen holds on to my guitar. I need to bounce and follow Eury. I run down the steps of the club. Pops follows close behind.

"Hold on!" Pops stops me from running out on the street. "Take a deep breath. We'll hail a cab and get you there."

He blows a loud whistle and a cab shows up in no time. I can barely figure out what to do with myself. He directs me to the back seat of the car.

Damn. I replay the scene in my head. How Eury fell and there was nothing I could do. I need to know she's okay. This cab isn't going fast enough.

"What happened, son?" Pops asks me again. I shake my head. How do I begin?

"Eury said there was this . . ." I hesitate. I can tell Pops anything. I know he won't judge. If anyone believes in unexplainable things, it would be him. Yet, I still can't formulate the sentences.

I punked out before. I can't repeat my mistakes.

"Eury said a spirit followed her from Puerto Rico to Tampa to here," I say. "I didn't believe her at first, Pops. I doubted her. Shunned her even when I actually saw the spirit with my own eyes."

My head hurts from this pain.

"¿Un espíritu?" Pops shakes his head. He goes quiet as he deciphers this revelation. "And you saw it?"

I turn to him. "Yes. It was a boy. I saw him. Barefoot. He was there on the roof. There was a flash, Eury fell, and the spirit was gone."

"You sure it wasn't a boy from around here?"

"I don't know. No. He wasn't from here. He wasn't real," I say. "Eury was scared. She kept saying he wanted to take her. He calls himself Ato."

"Ato." Pops repeats the name.

I pound on the driver's window. Tell him to go faster.

"When she first told me about Ato, I thought it was PTSD from the hurricane. Dad, he was on the roof. He took her."

"Okay," he says with the most serious face. "Let me think."

While Pops does that, my mind races, and I absentmindedly start to recall Lincoln Hospital's history. Lincoln was first called "The Home for the Colored Aged," a place where former slaves could find services in their old age. When the hospital relocated from Manhattan to the Bronx, they renamed it after the president. In the seventies, the Latino activist group the Young Lords took over the hospital, demanding better service for the community. Back then the doctors there were considered butchers. They still haven't lived down that reputation.

There are 347 hospital beds in Lincoln. One of the beds is where Eury lies.

Pops alerts the driver to pull in front of the entrance of the hospital. He gets out first. "I'll wait out here for you," he says. "Got to make some calls."

There's so much anger in this building. I'm adding to it because every single person I ask about Eury gets my fury. No one gives me a straight answer. I keep being sent from one window manned by a disgruntled worker to another. This woman right now tells me I have to be a relative to see her.

"I'm her brother," I lie. She reluctantly directs me to the third floor.

The waiting room is crowded. Every seat taken by Penelope's family. Aaron tells me Eury's mom is on her way.

"Has anyone seen her?"

He shakes his head. I can't stay here. I need to see her myself. Once I do, I can work out how best to help her. I leave before anyone starts asking me questions about what happened.

The hallways are endless. Eury is on the floor where they hold those in critical condition. Making sure the coast is clear, I open the first door. I apologize to the body lying there. I go to the next room. I know this isn't right, but I keep doing it. After the fourth try, I finally find her. Eury.

She's hooked up to machines making eerie sounds. The room is cold. How can she find her way back when there is nothing here reminding her of where she belongs?

"I'm so sorry, Eury. I messed up."

I lay my hand atop hers. Her fingers are swollen from the needle feeding into her vein. Someone has placed a rosary around each of her wrists. The rosaries are small, circular, with tiny beads and a dangling silver cross.

Where are you, Eury? Where did Ato take you?

"Sir, you are not allowed in here." The nurse has a weary face. She's had this argument before. Can't she see I'm different?

"I just want to see her for a second," I beg.

"No, sir. Don't make me call security," she says. "Let us do our job."

"What's wrong with her?" I ask the nurse.

"You'll have to wait for the doctor, who will speak to her family."

The nurse refuses to answer any more questions. She offers no details. Not a single thing. If Eury is connected to the machines, then she must still be alive. She's not completely gone.

Before I leave, I grab one of Eury's rosaries. It will be my link to her.

My head keeps remembering Ato's words. *You're too late.*

He's wrong. Eury will find a way out of Ato's hell. There has to be a way.

The nurse gently pushes me out the door. She points to where the elevators are. I try to compose myself. I'm not going to the waiting room. The waiting room is purgatory where people stand by for bad news to arrive. Eury will wake up. She has to.

I lean against the wall and cradle my head. What should I do? How can I help her? I'm so lost. The elevator door opens. I let my lead feet take me.

Outside the hospital is an endless night. There is a slight chill in the air as if the weather is also feeling the depth of my despair. It may be late, but the streets are filled with people. Tragedy is a magnet.

"Did you see her, son?" Pops leans against a mailbox. He hands me a bottle of water. How many hours have passed? It seems like an eternity.

Pops wraps his arms around me. I try not to choke up again.

"She looked like she's sleeping," I say. "It can't be right. This doesn't feel like real life."

"Let's go. If this spirit took Eury, there are people who may be able to help you," he says. "I'm going to take you to las casitas."

Las casitas. Is Pops talking about the blue house on Brook Avenue? He took me there once to listen to the Puerto Rican musicians play el cuatro. The house was crowded with people from the neighborhood singing Christmas songs. I remember it being cold outside, but inside the casita the warmth of everyone made it seem as if we'd been transported to a Caribbean island. What do las casitas have to do with anything?

Pops leads the way.

The faces of the people on the streets seem so strange to me. Then it dawns on me why. The old people, the viejitos and abuelas, stare at me. They meet my eyes and then turn in the direction of las casitas. Do they know where I am heading, where my father is meant to take me? They are pointing me to where I need to go.

No, I must be seeing things, tripping.

Casita Rincón Criollo stands out in this neighborhood. There's no way of missing it. The simple bungalow is painted completely in blue like the crystalline ocean of the Caribbean. Pops stops in front of the house and faces me.

"We are entering a whole other universe where the rules are different. Do you understand?" he says. "I am only in the peripheral, not as well-versed as the others. Are you open to this?"

I can't process the words Pops is saying, but I nod my head anyway.

"Wait here."

He knocks softly on the door before entering. A soft glow spills from underneath the door. The strong smell of tobacco fills the air. I think of Eury. What makes me think I can do anything to save her? Who am I to dare? Me. A dumbass from Manhattan. And yet, I find myself standing in front of this house with the hope that those inside hold a key to her. They must.

Eury, don't give up on me.

"Come in." A woman's voice. I open the door.

The small house is crowded with people. A bottle of rum is in the center of a table. Some of the people are familiar, faces I've seen around the neighborhood. Some are even part of Pops's bike crew. I recognize a lady who sat by Eury at the church. Here, she is different. I let her hold me even though I don't know her. Her hug reminds me of Grandma Lynn.

"This is Doña Petra," Pops says.

"We've been waiting," Doña Petra says.

A chill runs up my back. My mother's voice comes to me with a strict warning to stay away from these people. I can just imagine how she would look around this room and not approve. Even with Pops near, I am not sure if what I'm doing is right or if I'm going against my mother.

"Do you think Ato has power over her?" Doña Petra asks.

I turn to my father. Those in the room are already in this discussion. They are in the know.

Be open, my father said. I'm trying, but doubt is telling me to accept the reality that Eury fell and is in a coma and I have no business trying to change that. My mother's voice in my head is telling me to stick to what I know—singing, playing guitar, and reality.

"Eury said they used to be friends," I say. "She's known him since they were little."

"Do you know what he is?" A man with a scruffy beard speaks. He is the owner of the bodega a few blocks from here.

"I don't know," I say. Do I tell them what I really think? That this is an elaborate hallucination affecting both Eury and me.

"He's lying." A young mother sits rocking a sleeping baby. She says this with such bluntness. I'm being interrogated like I was earlier by the cops. Exhaustion hits me. My life is a constant battle of explaining myself. I pause for a moment, not knowing what to say.

They wait. "He's a spirit who wants to take Eury to the Underworld," I say. "That's what Eury told me."

"He doesn't believe," the old man says. I can't even correct him, because where is the lie?

"Ato has attached himself to Eury because of her light," Doña Petra says. "He's fed on this light for years with the conviction that soon they will be together in el Inframundo. The Underworld. That's where Ato has taken her."

She says this so matter-of-factly, like this piece of information should be obvious.

"What is a spirit if not the result of a colonized, traumatic state?" the man with the beard says. "Plant yourself in the mindset of the Taínos when they first saw the conquistadores arriving on the island. They were seeing things they never witnessed before. So much pain, and this pain can manifest in many ways."

They talk to me with calm voices, but what they are saying sounds impossible. I'm meant to be open, but how can I be when what they speak of is straight out of a horror movie? I'm dealing with a history of tragedy that goes back centuries.

"But how can I help her?" I ask.

Doña Petra shakes her head.

"You can't."

"Then why am I even here?" I head to the door. This is some bullshit. Why did Pops bring me here if the only thing these people will offer me is a history lesson? Don't tell me about the why. I need to know how. Give me the tools; if not, get out of my way.

My father presses his hand on my chest, preventing me from leaving.

"He believes there is still time," Pops says. "His heart is true. I've seen them. Eury and Pheus. I know they were meant to stand beside each other. Let him try."

"You abandoned her once," Doña Petra says. "You're too young to see what is plain. You should go back to singing at the club for your friends. It's an easier life."

I push Pops away. Let them stay in their shack. Eury is in an underworld with a ghost full of pain. They are like every adult out there. Like my Mom, who sees only the future me making money. Like my Father, who wishes only to see me using my music to heal.

"Screw this. I'll find another way." My hand is on the doorknob.

"Wait."

Doña Petra approaches me with an intense stare I cannot hold. "There is only one way to help Eury, but the entrance to el Inframundo will not be cheap. What are you willing to give up?"

"I don't have much." I sound like an idiot. I barely have an education. My father doesn't have a job. I'm broke.

"Dig deep," Doña Petra says. "Because your love will not be enough. Your anger will not be enough. What do you have of value compared to a tempestuous spirit who came from a world filled with suffering?"

Eury told me I can move mountains if I want to. She said this when I first met her. She whispered this the first night we kissed. They were sentences with such sustenance.

"He can sing," my father says.

"I heard you sing in church," Doña Petra says. "You do not believe in your own talent. What makes you think your voice is strong enough to open the doors to the Underworld?"

She is right. I ain't nothing. But what else do I have to offer?

"Let me try," I say. "Please."

Someone produces a guitar. It's old and out of tune. My fingers can't seem to remember how to strike a chord. I'm so nervous. I'm auditioning to see if I got what it takes to travel through space and time for Eury. My throat is parched. It feels like years since I sang on that stage. So little time has transpired, and yet it feels like a lifetime.

I sing the song "Adore." I close my eyes and channel all the love I have into the verses. I sing so the lyrics reach her, wherever she is. This is for Eury. She's lost and alone out there. I can help her. I will.

Although this sorrow of mine can fill galaxies, I surrender it and pour the anguish I feel into Prince's lyrics. I sing until I have nothing left inside.

My voice will save her.

CHAPTER 24

Eury

The juice from the mango drips down my fingers. It follows the curves and angles of my hand. The smell is sweet. I squeeze the fruit harder, and the fibrous pulp covers my palm.

"Aren't you going to eat that?"

Ato's cheeks are filled with the treat.

"No," I say. The river beckons me. I drop the messy remains. It is a small offering to the birds hovering above us.

I dive into the warm river. The strings from the mango float away. A tiny waterfall breaks from the rocks. I lie on my back and allow the sun to kiss me. How wondrous it is to be here.

Ato joins me. The bridge of his nose and cheeks are a little bit red. Glowing. He, too, lies on his back. We are both weightless, allowing the ripples from the waterfall to caress our bodies.

I dunk my head in the water. My long hair pulls on my back like a thick rope. Ato's curls are untamed. I search for his hand.

We fall asleep on a large flat rock. The birds form a circle around us and stand guard. Or that is what they seem to be doing. When I close my eyes, I don't dream.

Awake, my head rests on Ato's chest. He smells of coconut.

My Ato.

"Wake up." I tug at his curls. He nuzzles against my neck. The sound of the waterfall lulls us back to sleep.

This time it is Ato who taps my shoulder. The area is empty except for the birds. It is ours. No one can take it away from us.

"You must be hungry," Ato says. He stands and offers his hand. I take it.

"It's funny," I say. "I'm not. Maybe I will be later."

The birds are no longer in a circle. They are in a straight line. Our little winged army.

"The llorosas are visiting us again," I say.

Ato doesn't respond, and I'm left wondering if I'm mistaken.

"I know what will help." He leaves and runs to the bush, which is lush and green. His back and arms are thin but muscular. Ato has the body of a boy who has always worked outside.

He disappears into the bush, and I count to ten backward.

"If he doesn't return by the time I reach one, you will protect me, won't you?" I ask the leader of the birds. The small gray llorosa cocks its head to the side.

Ato soon appears with a beautiful, gleaming smile. He eats a sugarcane and offers me a piece. I push it away.

"Don't you like sugarcane?"

"Stop offering me things to eat," I say. "I'm not hungry."

"Let's take a walk, then," he says. "Maybe that will help with your appetite."

I feel out of sorts. It's not only the hunger that is missing. I can't quite place it.

"Am I supposed to be doing something?" I ask him.

Ato smiles. He has the longest eyelashes. "No. We're free to do whatever you want."

He is like the river, beautiful and wondrous. We walk away from the replenishing waters, and Ato leads me toward our house in the mountains. He caresses my back.

The wooden door to the house is open. We use a bucket of water to wash away the dirt on our feet before entering. A towel was left on the porch to dry our toes. Inside, everything is right where we left it. Simple living room furniture. A kitchen with a table right by a window so I can stare out at the flamboyán blooming so vibrantly. The bedroom we share is to the left. A small bathroom just off to the side of it. Our home.

It takes a few minutes for the shower to warm up. I wait while Ato hums a tune.

"You take a shower first," I say. "Don't hog the hot water."

"What if I do?" he teases.

I sit in the living room, the door still open. I can hear the llorosas by the tree. They rustle and fly about. A delicious breeze enters the house, and I relish it.

"Your turn," Ato says. He shakes his head, sprinkling water over me. I gently push him away.

In the bathroom, Ato has left me a single hibiscus in a glass of water. I take a long shower and rinse off the day spent in the river from my hair and body. When I'm done, I tuck the hibiscus behind my ear. I wear a flowing yellow dress. Barefoot, I walk to Ato, who stands by the kitchen.

"I have to step out now. I'll return," he says. "You want to start dinner while I'm gone?"

"Okay," I say. "Don't stay too long. Come back quick."

"I'll be back before dark." Ato pecks me lightly on the cheek before leaving. "I'll bring you something sweet."

The tiled kitchen floor feels good against my feet. The refrigerator has exactly what I need. Onions. Peppers. Cloves of garlic. Tomatoes. The knife glides effortlessly across the skin of the onion. I try my best to chop small enough pieces so when I place them in the pan, they will sizzle right away. The aroma fills the room. I pull back the curtain from the window and turn down the stove now that the water is boiling. Ato'll be famished when he returns. Maybe by then, I'll be hungry too.

Before I have any chance to worry, Ato enters holding bright yellow carambolas.

"Look what I found," he says. "They are ripe, ready to eat."

"Star fruits. They are so pretty." I place them in a bowl and set the rest on the kitchen table. "Where did you go?"

"Not far. Just making sure everything is in order," he says. "The food smells so good. I'm starving."

He serves me a large plate of food. Then he serves himself. I watch him eat. It feels good to cook for him, to do something for the person I love.

"You need to eat, Eury," he says. "Why aren't you eating? It's important."

I look down at my untouched plate. I take a forkful and stare at the grains of rice and the chunks of chicken. "I don't know."

"If you don't eat, you will get sick, and we will no longer be together. You have to eat. Don't you want to stay with me?"

"More than anything," I say. "I'm just not hungry."

He's disappointed in me.

"I'm sorry, Ato."

I leave him to eat his food in peace. I don't know what's

wrong with me. Maybe I'm nervous. Stress can make a person lose their appetite. It will return. I hope.

I walk to our bedroom and lie down. Ato eventually joins me. If I close my eyes, time will stop, and we won't worry about how I'm failing this test. He wraps his arms around my waist.

"Don't worry, Eury," he says. "We'll try later. Rest for now."

It's hard to relax when this silence is so eerie. I don't trust it.

"Ato, why can't I hear the coquís? It's dark out," I say.

The tiny frogs have always greeted me when the day breaks and night turns. This is an ominous sign. I sense a trap forming around our hearts.

"They are out there. Listen. You can hear them." Ato presses his lips and makes their singsongy sound.

I strain to hear the frogs. Instead, a llorosa cries out, and a shiver crawls up my arm.

Where did the coquís go?

CHAPTER 25

Pheus

Jaysen doesn't get it.

"We need you at the hospital," Jaysen says. "You were the last person to see her. People are starting to talk."

"Let me get the guitar." It's hard to control my anger. It's not Jaysen's fault. He's worried just like I am. We're both on edge. I can't tell him what I'm about to do. My head is still spinning since leaving Casita Rincón. I need to keep moving forward.

Jaysen hands over my piece.

"Swear to me right now on your abuela's grave that you'll stay close to Eury," I say. "I will kill you if you don't."

"Bro, I swear on everything holy. I'll stick close to Eury. But 'mano, tell me what you getting into so I can help."

I grab his arm and pull him in for a tight hug. My heart

thumps like it's about to jump out of my chest. I want Jaysen to come with me, but those in las casitas said this journey was mine alone to take.

"I'll see you soon."

"Okay, be careful. What's that shit your Pops always says? Be safe. Don't be stupid."

Jaysen walks back to the hospital. I hail a cab and go over what was said in las casitas. I'm so not prepared.

"There is so much for you to overcome," Doña Petra said. "The gods will not make it easy."

The elders in Casita Rincón schooled me on what was up. They said Eury is lost in the Underworld. To gain entrance into that world, I will have to entreat the gods. There are three who hold sway in el Inframundo. The first is Charon. He is the bridge between el Inframundo and our world. He must cross me over. Then there is Dīs Pater, the God of Wealth.

"Everything new in this city has ties to Dīs," the old man said. "The condos. The new supermarket. Even the club Dīs-traction. They say religion is the opium of the masses. I say money is the drug, and the gods are handing it out like water. Beside him, you will find Guabancex, the Goddess of Chaos. She holds Eury's fate. She is the ruler of the Underworld, the center of the hurricane."

They spoke to me of these wild things, and all I could do was try to commit the information to memory. The people in las casitas have been about this life for years. Generations upon generations knowledgeable about gods and their hooks on men. As for me, it is straight-up absurd. Those in las casitas think I don't have much of a chance. I need to try, tho.

I hold tight to the church pamphlet Doña Petra gave me. Inside the pamphlet are various prayers and simple Taíno symbols. Greetings to the gods, she said. I fold the pamphlet and tuck it back into my pocket.

"Are you a believer?" Doña Petra asked before I left.

I told her the truth. I had to.

"I want to believe," I say. "This is all new to me."

"They will use your lack of faith to their advantage," she said. "Think of the things you are afraid to lose. They will know."

"Tell him before he goes," the old man said.

Doña Petra hesitated. "Eury está viva pero pronto tendrá hambre."

Eury was still alive! I knew it the minute I saw her lying there on the sterile hospital bed that she wasn't gone.

"If she tastes their food, Eury will remain in el Inframundo," Doña Petra said.

"How much longer?" I asked.

"No mucho," she said. "Apúrate que el tiempo se te escapa."

Time escapes me. If I stop to think about what was said and what happened even for just a second, I will question everything. I can't. Pops waits by the Kingsbridge Armory.

I head back to the scene, back to the place where Eury was taken.

Club Dīs-traction.

Evil lurks in every crevice of this place. It lingers and becomes a beacon for the dead, an entryway to the bridge that connects earth to el Inframundo. This is how Doña Petra explained it to me.

As I approach the massive armory, my anxiety increases. Somewhere within the building, I must make contact with Charon. The cab stops at one end of the immense structure. Pops waits for me at the corner.

"You have your guitar," Pops says when I greet him. "Good. Let's go."

Some at Casita Rincón argued Pops shouldn't accompany me to the start of the journey. Doña Petra disagreed.

"He knows the way."

I was so confused when she said that. What else do I not know about Pops? I need information, and I don't think a church pamphlet with a few verses is going to help. We walk at a steady clip toward the entrance of the club.

"You've been to el Inframundo before."

"Not directly," he says. "I've led people to the bridge."

"How come I don't know this about you? I mean, what the hell," I say, raising my voice because this endless night continues to bring up disturbing surprises. "This is kind of a big deal. Maybe I should have been made aware of how you are connected to spirits?"

Pops stops walking. He stares intensely at me. I am acting out of pocket, but then, who cares? Everything is out of pocket. From seeing Ato to losing Eury to the folks in las casitas to me even entertaining the idea of el Inframundo existing. To find out Pops has a connection to this is almost too much to bear.

"My travels to the bridge have been dictated and led by violence and pain. They are personal to the individuals I guide to their final place. It is not on me to share their journey with you or anyone," he says. "I will be honest with you—only the dead go to el Inframundo. You are going against the grain. You understand?"

He is firm with me, not angry but direct, and yet I still feel as if I'm in trouble. I grew up not believing in any of this to now find out my own father has ties to the unexplainable. I shouldn't be going after Eury. I know nothing but a few chords and some bachata songs.

"How am I going to do this?"

"With this." He points to my heart.

I let out a loud sigh. I'm going to fail.

"Do you trust your father?" Pops lifts my chin up. "I promise to lead you to Charon. What they said en las casitas is true. Think of your history books, the evil caused by men. The misery only magnifies where we are heading. It manifests in things too horrific to describe. I'm not sugarcoating it. I'm afraid for both of us."

I shake my head. I don't think Pops understands how pep talks are meant to go.

He digs in his pocket and pulls out the ceramic elephant always situated by the apartment door.

"Every day, you touch this before entering the apartment. You've been doing this ever since you were a little kid. The elephant is meant to bring you good luck. Continue to acknowledge the gatekeepers and show them respect," he says. "You have strength flowing from you. Your ancestors will be with you, as will I. Find solace in this. What do you have of Eury's?"

I show him the small rosary I took when I went to see Eury at the hospital.

"Your name is Orpheus," he says. "Remember your gift."

No one ever really calls me Orpheus. The only person who called me that was Grandma Lynn in North Carolina. When I last saw Grandma Lynn, she could barely see. Moms said the cancer was taking over. She was the first person close to me to become sick. I was so timid around her, like I was afraid anything I said or did would contribute to her suffering. When I said my goodbyes, Grandma Lynn said to me: "You are named after Orpheus, who was a powerful singer and poet. You will be a beautiful singer too."

Here is Pops invoking the moment in Grandma Lynn's bedroom when she blessed me.

"I will. I'll remember where I came from." The tiny ceramic elephant is now secure in my pocket beside the church pamphlet and Eury's rosary.

We press on.

It's almost 4:30 in the morning. The streets are empty except for the occasional straggler. Workers heading home from a late shift. A dressed-up couple laughs, entering an apartment building. A man nods a hello to us before walking by. Soon, Dīs-traction comes into focus. There are no crowds lined up or bodyguards holding them back. The neon sign is unlit.

I shake my shoulders and roll them a bit. I look down at my shoes and wish I had time to change into Timbs. Dress shoes do not instill confidence. I try to rub out the dried bloodstains sprinkled throughout my suit but there's no point. I'm entering the unknown as is.

"Ready?" Pops asks.

The Kingsbridge Armory is so large, two full-sized football fields could fill the drill floor. The armory was once used to store weapons, bombs, and ammunition. Over the years, the place has hosted boxing fights and a four-hundred-foot shooting range. Residuals of violence can be found in every brick, and I'm walking right into it. So be it. Eury doesn't belong here or down in el Inframundo. And that's the truth.

"Yes, I'm ready. Let's do this."

I walk up to the door of the club only to find it unlocked. This scares the shit out of me because it means whoever is behind the door is surely expecting visitors.

"Hello?" I say. Pops follows behind.

The chairs are not up on the tables like they would be in most restaurants after closing. An uneasy feeling fills the air, a denseness I can't place. One overhead lamp beams from the now-empty restaurant. I walk toward it.

A hostess appears from within the darkness. She wears the same uniform from earlier in the night and carries a glass filled with what looks like red wine.

"We are here to see Charon," I say.

Something's amiss. As she draws nearer, the horror takes shape. Once she passes the overhanging spotlight, I get a good look at her.

"Oh my god," I say. Tremors take over my hands, spreading to my arms, my legs.

The server is missing a jaw. Half her face is torn off. Bones and crusted, bloody skin hang loose. Her eyes match the blood.

Behind me, Pops mutters to himself. A prayer. A spell. I don't know.

I never prayed before.

No. That's not true. When my parents told me they were separating, I prayed that night. I thought it was my fault they couldn't stay together. Every kid does this. They go through all the times their parents argued and make a list of when they were in the center of that argument. My list wasn't long, but still.

While I heard my father pack up his things, I lay in my bedroom praying he would change his mind. I didn't even have any idea who I was praying to. I swore to listen and stop fooling around if this god would keep my parents together. Foolish promises any kid would make.

How will prayers help me now?

CHAPTER 26

Eury

When Ato sleeps, he looks like an angel, and yet as I lie beside him, I am restless. I do my best not to wake him. The sky slowly lightens. Day will break soon. I grab a blanket and wrap myself with it. I step outside in search of the coquís.

The coquís aren't the only things missing. Although there is an abundance of vegetation and greenery, no insects can be found. No mosquitos. No flies. No bees. None. It's not possible to eat ripe fruit without bugs to pester you. Nothing here quite makes sense. I shouldn't complain. I know I shouldn't be looking for faults, but I feel imbalanced, unsure. The ground doesn't seem sturdy enough to keep me erect.

This silence feels so strange. Are we isolated from others?

How is that even possible? Where are the people? Have they found their own piece of paradise, hidden from view?

I continue to walk. Not too far away. I don't want to alarm Ato. He's been so patient with me. The colors from the blooming flowers seem otherworldly. It is as if a painter worked overnight while we slept to highlight each petal with a vibrant tone. It doesn't seem real.

Perhaps I am unworthy of such beauty. If I am only searching for mistakes, maybe I am the one who doesn't belong here. I need to let go of this weakness. There is nothing wrong with this life, this place. I have a home and Ato beside me. What more can I ask?

I pluck a few flowers to bring inside. I want Ato to know I appreciate everything he does. I will try harder to enjoy my surroundings and let go of this apprehension.

As I approach the house, I see him. His back is to me. Even from where I stand, I can tell his muscles are tense.

"What are you doing?" I ask as I join him. Ato stares up at our tree.

"They are not supposed to be here," he says.

The llorosas stare down at us. Their wings serve as coats. Hundreds of them line the branches of the large tree. Whenever I see them, I only feel peace.

"They are not bothering us. They keep me company while you are away."

Ato searches for a wooden stick. I try to grab it away from

him, but he is too quick. He takes one large swing against the trunk of the tree. The birds take to the sky, their wings making a thunderous sound.

"Why, Ato?"

"They are not meant to be here."

"Are we supposed to be here? You sound ridiculous."

I turn away from him. He follows me into the house.

"Get away from me. It's hard to talk to you when you act this way," I say. "The llorosas are tiny. What can they do to us?"

Ato tries to hold me.

"Why are you so troubled? Isn't being here enough? Being together?" he asks. "This place has everything you ever wanted. What did I overlook? Tell me."

He takes a carambola from the bowl I placed on the kitchen table. He cuts a large piece and dangles it in front of me.

"Here, Eury. This will make you forget the birds." He urges me to eat. My dread feels like a growing pit in my stomach. Like a virus. A cancer.

I hold the piece of fruit. Everything about it is perfect, from its strong citrusy smell to the pulp filled with juice. I'm not hungry. Not even a little bit.

The leader of the llorosas appears in the kitchen window. In my mind I have invented a whole life for her. She is a fearless leader protecting her flock. We are connected somehow.

I don't know how, but I know this to be true. The llorosas are the only animals I see out here. Perhaps we met in another lifetime. Perhaps I was once a llorosa soaring in the sky in search of others to protect. Maybe I was lost and she found me. The llorosa tilts her head, giving me a quizzical look.

Ato is wrong. There is nothing malicious about this bird.

I place the fruit on the palm of my hand and offer it to the bird. The bird is reluctant, but eventually she props herself close to my palm and pecks at the fruit. She doesn't hurt me with her pointy beak.

"No!" Ato flies into a rage. He reaches for the bird. The llorosa escapes toward our tree. Ato runs outside, and I chase him.

"Leave her alone. She's not hurting us."

Ato doesn't answer. It is as if he's become possessed. I grab his hand. He shoves me to the ground. He swings at the llorosa with the wooden stick. He misses. Ato swings again, this time making contact. The stick hits the bird in midflight. She goes down.

I scream.

Ato turns to face me. He no longer has an angelic face. His eyes are completely black. He is unrecognizable, transformed and mutated. A monster.

He holds the cane, raised above his head, about to strike at the bird again.

I run inside, grab the knife, and rush toward him.

"Leave the bird alone!" I aim the knife. "I don't know you. I don't know a thing about you. Get out of here!"

Ato drops the stick. His face slowly returns to the person I am familiar with, but I can still see remnants of his true nature. He drops to his knees. Tears stream down his face. I don't believe them. This is all part of an elaborate act. My hand stays firmly clasped around the knife.

"Eury. I would never harm you," he pleads. His voice rings like a chorus. A melody meant to calm my temper. He will do the same to me as he did to the llorosa. "Please believe me. I'm only protecting you. Us."

"I don't recognize you or this place," I say.

I look at the house. This is where I grew up. Every object in this home is one I've seen before, and yet it feels like an empty shell. None of it rings true.

"Don't come near me."

Ato pleads. I hold steadfast. I will not break.

The jawless server draws nearer, and I want to run. Pops is behind me. His presence gives me a bit of courage, enough for me to stay.

"We're here to see Charon." I sound like a weakling no matter how much I try to come off as hard. Blood drips from the hostess's mouth. She keeps coming.

More servers appear. Jawless men and women. Bodyguards missing half their faces. Skin falling off. They show themselves along the bar, by the tables. Hundreds of them. The men are tall, every single one cut to the bone. No shirt to flex what's what. These faceless creatures, beasts, are gunning for us. I don't have a weapon, not a damn thing but a guitar. Like a fool, I raise my fists. I will punch whoever comes close.

"Tell Charon Apolo wants to see him," Pops says. "I seek passage for my son."

The jawless things completely surround us. My chin is raised up. If I go down, I'll take 'em with me. But my fists are trembling, and I notice the rapidness of my breathing. Pops places his hand over my fists and lowers them.

"Don't even think about it. You will be devoured and become one of them."

"So what the hell do we do?"

"We wait."

The jawless creatures bump against me. They egg me to make the first move. There is a stench of rotten, burning flesh. Bile rises up in me. There is a frenzy. The things want to tear into us, and they will. It's only a matter of time. I hold Eury's prayer bracelet in my hand and the elephant statue in the other. I squeeze them both tight.

From behind a velvet curtain, a man materializes, completely unkempt, with a scraggly beard and wild eyes. His jaw is intact. He wears piles of clothes in shades of brown and holds a cane made of gold. If I would have seen him out in the streets, I wouldn't have even thought to look his way. He looks like every homeless person I've seen before in New York. The only difference is this man exudes authority. He is the leader of these gruesome creatures, so the wide smile he displays only makes me shudder even more.

"It's been a minute, Apolo. Who is it you got with you?"

Charon says. "He smells a little too unripe, not done enough for passage."

Behind Charon is Sileno, the owner of Dīs-traction, with a bandage wrapped around his head. Seeing his ugly horse face brings everything into focus. I want to kick his ass for whatever he did to Eury.

"Ahh, el Nuevo Nene de la Bachata. This boy can sing," Sileno exclaims. "How's Eury doing?"

"Come closer, and I'll show you exactly how she's doing," I say. "Deadass."

Sileno snickers, and that just pisses me off even more. I go to bum-rush him, but Pops holds me back.

The jawless men step aside. This allows Charon to take a closer look at me. He smells of rotting flesh too. Is that what he's concealing underneath all the layers?

"You can't pass unless you are dead," Charon says. "Easy enough. We've got you covered."

Charon pulls out a machete from underneath his long, tattered coat. The machete is covered in dried blood. His army waits for his bidding. They sway back and forth like boxers standing by for the first-round bell to ring.

This is it? I'm going down at this moment? Naw. This journey just started. Charon is going to take me across. I'm on a mission, and the leader of this death army is just part of this story. Doña Petra said to remember my name. I am Orpheus, and I can move mountains.

My father always taught me to stare at your opponent to let them know you are human. "Look them in the eyes. No matter what class, you are two men bound to walk this earth together." But Pops also said to pay respect to the gatekeepers. Charon's got all the cards. I am a nothing player, so I drop to my knees.

"I'm not worthy to be here, to be among your people," I say. "There is a girl who was not meant to have crossed over. Her name is Eury. Ato took her way before her time."

At the mention of Ato, Charon lowers the machete. He doesn't put it away. I can see from the corner of my eye the blade is beside him.

"This is your domain," I say. "Ato is trying to sneak one over on you."

"Nobody gets past me," Charon says.

He uses the tip of the machete to prove his point right on my shoulder. The tip manages to pierce through my suit and into my skin, but I don't flinch. I take the pain.

"He speaks the truth," Pops says. "Ato took the girl before her time."

"Just ask ese palomo cara de caballo," I say. "Sileno knows what's up."

"Me? No. I was too busy with the club," Sileno says, "tending to customers—"

"Speak!" Charon yells. Sileno sheepishly stares at the floor. He is no longer the lengua larga horse face from earlier.

230

"Ato entered the Bronx a couple of days ago. Heard he's been obsessed with Eury for years, from back when she lived in Puerto Rico," Sileno says. "I didn't understand why until I met her."

A beat goes by. Then another. Charon chews on this revelation.

"Ato." Charon says his name with as much hate as I have.

"I need to find Eury before it's too late," I say. Charon has to cross me over.

"Ato thinks he's above it all because he's beloved by Guabancex and Dīs," Sileno says. "He's always getting his way."

"I don't care about that," Charon says. "What I want to know is why I should cross him?"

I slowly stand up. My head is still lowered in an act of reverence. Charon hasn't put away his blade. This is for Eury, because I'm being tested, and my only currency is my promise to find her.

I hold my guitar and get ready to sing.

Before I can even hit the first note, Charon grabs my instrument. He hands it over to one of his jawless soldiers. Fine. I don't need my guitar to confess my lamentations for Eury. I will sing my entreaty. I start.

"Cállate," Charon says.

I keep singing. This is what I have.

"Why do you bring me this basura, Apolo?" Charon asks. "He can't even sing."

Charon shoves me to the ground. I don't stop. I am insignificant here, but I will lift my voice until it reaches Eury.

The soldiers look back at Charon and then at me with their demonic eyes. They claw at my legs, my arms, and face. They draw blood. I keep doing what I do.

The master of this hell raises his machete again. Charon wants me to stop. I won't. I've been sent here for a reason. He wants to get rid of my jaw so I can no longer sing, so that I can join his mute soldiers. He can try, but this song has its own divination.

"Pheus is the only thing I've made that's pure." Pops chokes up. "Don't end his life simply because you refuse to acknowledge the good."

Charon and Sileno laugh at my father.

"Weren't you here when he performed? Didn't you see how much he loved the limelight? The only light your son wants is fame. It's why Eury ended up with Ato," Sileno says. "Take pride in knowing your son is just like you: a selfish failure."

I dart up. I swing right into Sileno's face. No one talks about my Pops like that, demon, god, or what have you. No one. Sileno drops to the floor. He laughs with a maniacal grin, blood now dripping from his nose.

"Let me do the honors, Charon," Sileno says. "Let me complete this young boy's destiny to serve you."

Charon flashes his stained teeth. Brown and yellowing.

"No. If you are going to perform," Charon says, "then you need to *really* perform."

Charon pounds the ground with his cane three times. The restaurant walls collapse inward. I cower to protect myself from being crushed by the rubble.

"Pops!" I yell before everything turns black.

I open my eyes to find I am on stage. My father sits at a center table with Charon and Sileno. Charon sucks on a hookah while Sileno drains his glass of red wine. All around the room, the tables are occupied with lechones, piglet devils with long, curved snouts and tall horns covered in tiny spikes. During Carnaval de Santiago in Santo Domingo, people dress as lechones in silk clothes adorned in sequins with their faces concealed under papier-mâché masks. But these lechones are not wearing masks. They are real. The lechones violently swing sisal ropes from their seats, slamming on the tables, grunting and slobbering.

Behind me, a fast bachata is being played. I turn to face the musicians backing me up. A demon piglet plucks rabidly at the strings of a guitar. Pieces of flesh fall from his fingers. The congueros bang with their eyes closed in ecstasy. Blood covers the skin of the congas.

Down on the dance floor, lechones huddle close to women. They twirl and twirl their partners to the rhythm of the demented bachata.

"No más, por favor," a woman pleads, begging to stop. I look down at her bare feet. They are bleeding.

"Ayúdame," another woman cries. Their demon partners cackle. The women raise their hands in supplication while being spun across the dance floor.

My heart breaks.

"I'm sorry," I say. "I'm so sorry."

"Sing!" bellows Charon.

CHAPTER 28

Eury

Ato slowly gets up. I won't succumb to his pleas.

"Eury. We are meant to be together," he says. "In time, you will accept this. I'm only protecting you."

"No!" His eyes are black coals. His face is a demonic mask. "Don't come any closer. You are not real. You're a nightmare, and I will wake up soon."

"No, Eury, don't do this," Ato begs. "I implore you. Don't shun me. You are mine."

I am his? I am a thing, a possession, like this house filled with familiar objects. Ato confirms my fears.

"I belong to no one," I say.

Ato's face shifts again from remorse to anger. He clenches his jaw.

"I will give you time but not long. A bit of space to change this way of thinking," he says. "Just remember, you are meant to be by my side for eternity."

He walks away. I stand clutching the knife until the dense brush overtakes his body and he is no longer visible.

The llorosa doesn't move. It's so small.

I cradle the bird in my hands. Her companions have not returned. I can't allow them to find her this way. I dig a hole into the soil big enough to contain the bird.

Wait.

I've buried a llorosa before. I try desperately to remember. When? When did this happen?

I close my eyes and search deep in my thoughts for this memory. There is an unmoving llorosa, and I am distraught. Who was with me at the time?

Think.

A hand on my shoulder comforted me as I wept. A person who cared for me. No, there was more than one person. And it wasn't here. It was in El Yunque. Ato had killed a llorosa in El Yunque. But who consoled me after his hideous act? If only I could lift the persistent fog blanketing my mind . . .

I place the llorosa into the hole and cover the bird with soil, saying a prayer not only for the llorosa but for guidance to get me out from under this unending horror. I am lost, but perhaps if I repeat the petition, I will find the right path.

A prayer to bring back lost memories. There are people who love me. Maybe they are thinking of me right now.

The once-dormant wind stirs. In the far distance, storm clouds form. The sudden change in the weather feels foreboding. I don't know why, but I can't be here when the storm reaches. I'm not safe. I must leave.

Inside, I find a backpack in a closet. I take a blanket and a change of clothes. These items are mine, but in a way they do not seem real. I place them into the backpack. I am afraid everything I touch will disintegrate.

I head to the river.

Masses of dark clouds seem to increase in size with every second. I see no one. Not an animal. Not a bird. This strange place can't be real.

I keep walking. It's hard to calculate the time. My body can't possibly survive without food or drink, and yet, here I am. The voices in my head continue to shrill, alerting me that this is all wrong. But I can't dissolve into inactivity. An answer lies somewhere. I will walk until I find it.

What would happen if I swam along the river? Would my body eventually give up after such a long stretch? There is nothing for me to swim to. Not a boat or a dinghy. I wish the llorosas would come back. At least they are familiar. Their chirps were a reminder of another time and place.

There must be someone else on this island. It is much too big to house only Ato and me. I will find a person to help get me away. Ato will do the same to me that he did to la llorosa. I can feel it.

The longer I walk, the more it feels as if I am barely making any headway. My legs ache. I need to stop. I sit down on the dirt, grab a handful, and let it sift through my fingers. I have to keep moving, but this tiredness weighs me down. If I rest for only a little bit, I should still be able to outrun the start of this storm. The dark clouds are still a ways from me. It's so hard for me to stay awake. I'm so tired.

Maybe if I rest for a second.

My eyes grow heavy. I give in.

A noise startles me awake. I'm no longer by the river. I'm back inside the house on the bed I share with Ato. The space beside me feels warm as if he just woke up. I turn to grab the knife I had tucked into my belt loop, but it is no longer there. Instead I am wearing a dress. It's hard to breathe.

I was by the river, walking away from the storm. This I remember. If I repeat these sentences, surely I will not give in to this delusion.

There is movement inside the house. Ato is here. He is the cause of this. I look around the room for a weapon, but the bedroom dresser has been stripped of everything. The walls are also bare.

I step out of the room to find Ato standing by the open front door, his back to me. If I run to the kitchen, will it be enough time to get the knife? No. It is too far away.

"I've put away the knives," Ato says as if he's reading my mind. "You won't need them."

I'm a prisoner here. There are no more tears left. I can walk for hours and still find myself right back where I started. Ato knew this. He let me play this game of hope. I won't cry or fall apart although my heart pounds out of control. I must remain calm.

"Why keep me here when I don't want to be with you?" I ask. "It's not right. Can't you see?"

He doesn't turn around.

"Do you remember when we first met? Your father had left you. You were so angry. You thought perhaps if you destroyed the gift he gave you then it would hurt him," he says. "You were so little. So you used a cane from this yard and started to hit the doll."

I slump down to the living room floor. My memories are not fully formed; they are only glimpses. Feelings. The anger I can remember. The tears that ran down my cheeks as I hit the doll I recall too. Mami was inside the house submitting to her own sorrow.

"It rained, but you refused to take cover," Ato continues. "Instead, you wished your father dead. I was with you."

I don't remember him sitting next to me or the rain. I only remember hitting the doll. I've blocked everything about Papi. How he looked in the mornings when he sat to drink his cafecito on the porch. How he liked to listen to his boleros loudly on Sundays while everyone went to church. Ato sprang from my anger. He came to me when I wanted to hate. What does

239

it mean to attract violence into your life? Is that what I'm meant to live with forever?

"You will eat today."

He turns to me. His face is erased. A blur. I can't make him out. I rub my eyes and try to see Ato for what he is, but it's not possible. It is as if I'm watching cuts of an unfocused movie.

"I don't want you to be sick anymore, Eury. To be in such pain," he says. "Unlike all the others, I will not abandon you. You see that now, don't you? This is all for you. No more sadness. We'll stay here forever as it was meant to be."

Forever. I weep until I feel nothing.

CHAPTER 29

Pheus

A rapid bachata vibrates and bounces off the walls, causing bottles to fall from the bar. The lechones snarl and whip their ropes in a frenzy. Pops covers his face with his hands to shield it from the lassos. The demon guitarist jabs me toward the microphone with his instrument.

"I can't," I say.

"We can't hear you," Sileno yells. The lechones growl along with him. "Louder!"

The air is thick with smoke from Charon sucking on the hookah. He pounds his fist on the table while the dancers wail in pain. I won't sing a bachata. I won't torture these spirits forced to dance with monsters.

"No," I say.

"Did he say no?" Sileno slaps my father on the shoulder. "Charon. I think he has doubts."

Charon stands up and places the blade against my father's neck.

My god. Please, don't do this. I don't want to play this game.

"Don't hurt him," I say. "I'll sing."

I inhale and try my hardest to stop from trembling. To find my voice once again. I'll do this but not the way Charon or Sileno expects. I walk over to the guitarist and press my hand over the strings. He snarls and snaps at me with his protruding jaw.

"Slow the hell down," I command. "Everyone slow down."

Charon keeps the machete by Pops's neck. I got to make this right.

I sing the first verse from "Pena por Ti," by Luis Segura. Amargue. A song of bitterness, of love lost. I can't sing of hate, so I will sing this heartrending tune.

The lechones whip with furious intentions, but eventually they calm down. Couples slow their maddening spins. The women still cry out but not as painfully as before. Their whimpering causes me to find my voice and join in their lament. The demons begin to sway to the music. They stop thrashing their ropes. Some even drop their heads onto the table. Sileno slams his fist to try to stir the demons, but he's out of luck. My voice has lulled the beasts to sleep.

Charon lowers the machete from my father's neck. When the song ends, not one word is uttered. The club is completely silent except for the dancers' barefoot shuffling and the snoring coming from the demons.

Within seconds, Charon leaps from my father's side to mine. He straddles me to the ground and raises his machete. I close my eyes. The machete lands just inches away from my face. The blade feels hot against my cheek. If I move, it will surely pierce my skin.

"What else you got?" Charon asks.

I clumsily dig in my pockets.

"I have this." In my hand, I hold the token my father gave me, the small statue of the elephant.

Charon snatches the ceramic piece and chuckles at the elephant's face. When he gets up, the lechones vanish, as does Sileno.

"Let's go," Charon says.

My guitar is on the floor, still intact. I strap it to my back.

Pops holds me longer than he should. I'm crying because I don't want to do this alone, but I must. He nods and wipes my tears. "Be safe. Don't be stupid."

I catch up to Charon, turning only once to see Pops still standing there.

CHAPTER 30

Eury

Ato fusses about in the kitchen. "I'm going to make us a feast," he says with a bit of pep as if everything has been decided.

"Please, Ato, let me go," I plead through my tears.

"You will eat before the storm reaches the house," he responds. He will soon force food down my throat, but I fear eating means I am bound to this place forever. I must find a way out of this jail.

Think.

The storm gathers momentum outside. Leaves from the palm trees begin to fall from the now-forceful wind. Rocks tap against the windows, louder as each minute passes. I walk back to the living room and stare at the rolling clouds. Darkness spreads.

A hurricane. There is a hurricane encroaching on the

island. I start to hyperventilate. The room spins. Oh my god. A hurricane is coming to tear this house apart like it did once before. My home. The walls came apart. I was with Mami, cowering in the bathtub. I remember it all so clearly now. We have to take cover.

Wait. This is not my real home, and Ato doesn't have control of this hurricane—does he? If Ato wants me to eat before the hurricane reaches us, that must mean the hurricane is on a timetable Ato is unable to steer.

Eury. Think.

The hurricane.

Maybe the answer can be found in the storm—the one thing Ato can't control. Instead of walking away from the dangerous gale, should I be heading right toward it?

The rain has changed into a torrential downpour. Tree branches shoot across the sky. The storm is so close now.

I don't know if I can do this. Go toward my greatest fear. My heartbeat pounds in my ears, almost drowning out the roar of the wind. I'm not strong enough. Fear of this hurricane will destroy me, as the storm itself destroyed my home.

But my fate hangs in the balance. I can either face the hurricane, or eat and stay with Ato forever.

Am I strong enough to do what I must?

Ato returns with a tray of food. Everything is laid out so elegantly, right down to the flowers in a clear vase placed at the center of the tray. He goes back to the kitchen and returns with a large glass of water. His face is still a blur.

Ato is a devil. I will run into the hurricane to get away from him. I must.

He conveniently leaves the utensils in the kitchen. I'm meant to eat with my hands like an animal. I pick up a perfect slice of mango, the brilliant orange-yellow color unmarked by bruises. This fruit is not for me. It will kill me.

"There was a song you used to sing," I say as sweetly as possible. I try not to look at him. If I do, my despair will overtake me and I won't be able to do what I have to do. "When I was scared of the thunderstorms. Do you remember?"

I don't know if this is true, but I am searching for any way to get out of here. Ato used to be my protector. This memory sits at the edge of my thoughts. I had affection for him not too long ago. I must dwell on this delicate memory of our relationship and hope it will be enough to fool him.

His face is still a fog. It is as if someone took an eraser and wiped his features clean. He is unfocused. I have to concentrate on keeping my breathing steady, otherwise the terror will become too much.

I risk a glance out the window and see the tree is now inhabited once again by llorosas. They have returned. The sight of them gives me courage.

"Sing for me, Ato. Mark this occasion with your voice."

I play against his vanity, and Ato can't resist. After all, he only wants me to worship him. Let him believe I will. Ato stands up, and I can see the front door is wide open behind him. It is so dark that we should turn the lights on, but Ato doesn't. He is too immersed in the idea of performing for his captive audience.

"This was your favorite," he says. "Do you remember?"

He begins, and the words are so familiar. The lyrics burrow inside me. I've heard this song sung before, but not by Ato—by someone who loves me. The memory is struggling to come forth, but it fills me with strength. It will thrust me forward through that open door.

Ato's face is still intangible. I lift the mango to my mouth like I'm about to eat it, and his voice becomes even more melodic. It is as if the house has been filled with millions of Atos singing from every corner. Multiple angels of death serenade me into joining them.

I won't.

As the song reaches its climax, I smile at Ato. This smile will be his undoing. Instead of taking a bite from the mango, I lift the tray with force, spilling its contents everywhere. Before the fruit hits the ground, I'm running out the door. Despite the commotion, Ato is right on my heels.

Outside, the winds blow out of control, pushing and pulling me every direction. The clouds are so dense, I can barely see.

"Eury, don't!" He grabs my arm, attempting to drag me

back inside. But the llorosas descend upon Ato in a giant swarm. He releases me, swinging at the birds violently.

I fight my way toward the storm. I am drenched, but I keep running into the void.

I remember who sang the song. His name is Pheus. He sang the song in Spanish, and when he did, it reminded me of home.

Pheus. He was the one who could move mountains with his voice, not Ato.

The wind picks me up and thrashes me to the ground. My knees are bleeding, but I stand. I keep running. I will journey into the center of this furor.

CHAPTER 31

Pheus

Steps lead up to what was once the drill floor of the armory. The area is under construction, soon to be turned into an ice-skating rink. I try my best to keep up with Charon's elongated strides. His machete stays hidden underneath his grungy layer of clothes.

In the corner, young Black and brown men appear in military uniforms. They are jovial and loud as they unload boxes from a van. A soldier opens one and pulls out a rifle, gleefully examining it as if he just received a Christmas gift. As we walk past them, I get a good view of the soldier. He looks like Tío Luis, my uncle who fell to drugs after too many deployments. He has the exact jawline, the bushy eyebrows similar to mine.

The last time Uncle Luis spoke to me, he was really drunk.

It was New Year's Eve. Everyone was huddled around the television, waiting for the ball to drop in Times Square. When it did, fireworks went off in the neighborhood, and Tío Luis suddenly grabbed my arm so tight I winced from the pain.

"Them devils want to kill us," he said, balling his other hand into a fist, ready to use it. "I'm not going down like that."

Pops gently pried my uncle's hand off me. He led Luis to another room to calm him down. A couple of years later, he was gone.

The soldier who looks like Tío Luis aims the gun and practices shooting.

This is horrible.

Charon chuckles.

"You don't like that, huh? There's so much to love in this building," he says. "So much history."

We pass more apparitions of soldiers in formation. They each have clean-shaven, innocent faces. Practically my age. The soldiers salute a flag, then they turn their heads in unison to stare at us.

"This way," Charon says.

More stairs. They spiral up and up. Charon taps at the Estigio sign with his cane and motions for me to continue. We are heading to the roof, back to the pool where this nightmare began.

The pool is completely drained of water. Police tape still

marks the bloodstains on the floor. Lights flick on, and the atrium opens. The waning moon shines brightly.

It's strange how I expect to see Eury smiling by the bar, with her palms out for me to hold. Ready to leave this all behind.

"You. There." Charon points his cane to the center of the empty pool. I do as he says and climb in.

"Remember when I told you that I only cross those who have died?" he asks. "It's true. In so many lifetimes, I've never made a mistake. Until Ato. He plays by his own rules, but no one is exempt. Eventually he will get what he deserves, and I will be eagerly waiting. It's the only reason why I'm letting you go."

Charon crouches down by the edge, holding the cane for support.

"Young love doesn't interest me. My domain is pain," he says. "But I'm not here for a spirit trying to get a cut of my fun."

"I'll take care of it," I say as if I'm being commissioned to take Ato out like John Wick or something. I'm talking out of my ass, and Charon's big grin only proves how out of my league I am.

"Right," he says in between laughs. "You and your guitar."

"Eury doesn't belong in el Inframundo, and neither do I. I'm going to find her, and we are going to bounce on out of there real quick." I say this more to myself than to Charon. "Life isn't only about anguish and grief. There's hope too."

"You consider yourself a poet. Don't you? I have a little poem for you." Charon clears his throat and places his hand over his heart. "*Through the straight pass of suffering the martyrs even trod.* Emily Dickinson. She knew about suffering. So does your friend Eury. So will you."

"I'm no martyr," I say.

"Sure. Now shhhhh." He places his finger to his mouth. "I hope you can swim."

He hits his cane three times on the floor, and with that, the pool begins to fill with water. I turn to run, but my feet are stuck to the tiled bottom.

The water seeps in quickly. It reaches my knees. My waist. Charon stares at me with a wide grin.

"Yo! I can't move my legs," I scream. "I can't swim if I can't move my legs."

It reaches my arms. My shoulders. It takes only seconds for the water to cover my neck.

"Not my problem," Charon says. "Have fun."

I inhale the largest gulp of air before my whole body is submerged. My heart is about to burst out from my chest. When I'm completely immersed in the water, I'm finally able to move. I propel myself to the surface, but a barrier stops me. An invisible wall of some sort. Charon waves from above. Shit.

I can't hold my breath for much longer. There has to be a way out.

Something bumps into me. No, it's not something. Someone. Bodies upon bodies float beside me. Bloated faces of people in uniform. Then more. They crash against me, surrounding me. I thrash and kick. They try to drag me down.

So many. I'm going to die here.

I push them away, but they keep coming. My lungs burn. I'm going to drown with these forgotten souls.

I can't. I won't.

I try one more time. I push them away and swim up to the surface, toward the brilliant moon. My fists pound against the invisible barrier.

Please. Let me live.

Hands pull on my ankles and my guitar from below. I keep hitting the barrier, but I feel myself slipping. Getting weak.

I think of family. Of my father and mother. Of Grandma Lynn and Uncle Luis. *Give me strength.*

I pound on the unseen wall with all my rage and fear. I'm swallowing water. I can't hold on for much longer. *Let me live.* One more punch is all I've got left. I throw it with everything inside of me.

The barrier disappears, and I grab the ledge of the pool and thrust myself over. I try to catch my breath. Spitting out water. Coughing my guts out. It feels like hours, but eventually I am able to sit up.

Charon is nowhere to be found. Everything is dark and empty. As for my clothes, they are completely dry. Not one drop on the guitar. As if my near-drowning was only a dream.

But I can't forget what I've seen—terrible things I never wanted to see. Reminders of people taken much too soon. The truth is ugly and violent. I've read history books, devoured them like they were candy. I can spit dates and statistics like no other. They were my weapons against anyone who thought they could revise what has happened. Now I am to bear witness to these historical consequences in real time. There's no hiding behind the pages of a book. The horrors are right in front of me in this realm where only the dead are allowed.

If I'm being shown this, then what horrors is Eury facing? She only needs to eat to be trapped here forever. What if I never see her again? What if my voice is not enough? I clutch the prayer beads and concentrate on reaching her.

If you're out there, Eury, hold on.

CHAPTER 32

Eury

Each step I take, I am pushed back toward the house by these violent winds. A heavy object slams into me. I fall on my back, but I grit my teeth through the pain. I can't stop.

"Eury, please! I made this for you," Ato yells. "Everything as you like it."

Ato has lied to me since I first saw him. A memory of us trickles in, the moment when I first met Ato, and I tried to destroy Papi's gift.

He won't come back because of what you did.

Ato's words cut as sharp as a knife, a wound that never healed. For so long, I believed Papi must have left because of something evil within me. But I was wrong. I was only a child. Ato wedged himself like a cancer, clinging to my grace. He fed me this lie, and I carried it with me everywhere.

I don't know exactly why Papi left. I may never really know. But I know now it was never my fault.

I turn and watch as the tumultuous wind tears the roof off the house. My god. I can't stop the memory from overtaking me, of cowering in the bathtub while my home, my real home in Puerto Rico, was destroyed around me. But this time, it's Ato who watches in anguish as his dollhouse is swept away by the storm.

Before I succumb to the nightmare of the past, I remember Pheus and his beautiful face. How he closed his eyes when he sang. His dimples. I remember his smile and how he turned so serious when he spoke of the histories of places and buildings. I remember the way his hands caressed my cheek when we kissed. *Pheus.*

These memories will launch me away from this hell.

I turn away and push forward with all my strength. I must reach the center of this hurricane.

Something yanks my shoulders back—Ato. We tussle to the ground.

"Don't leave me, Eury." Ato has the face of an angelic young boy. This evil tormentor. He will not have me.

I shove him with all I can muster and run. I only manage a few steps before the wind takes hold of my body, pulling me off the ground and tossing me toward the eye of the storm.

Branches and parts of the house come hurling toward me. I'm spinning and thrashing through the air. I watch as the roof careens forward. It will crash into me, and I will be torn apart. I can't stop the momentum.

The roof is upon me. I think of Pheus, when he sang "Adore" in Spanish.

Then, there is only black.

———

I don't open my eyes. Not yet. Will I find myself right back in my jail with Ato ready to feed me a deadly feast?

There is no noise. No wind howling. No voices. A void. Am I dead? Again?

I wiggle the toes on one foot first. Then the other.

I'm scared to wake up. I don't want to relive this nightmare. I wait. My breathing is certain. If I'm breathing, then surely I am still alive. Or is breathing nothing but a dream?

I open my eyes. It takes a moment for shapes to come into focus. But then I recognize where I am and start to cry.

El Yunque is as lush and green as I remember it. Verdant. My beautiful rainforest. How can a real place feel so otherworldly? When I first entered El Yunque, the sadness from Papi leaving was lifted in a way I can't really explain. It was different than my interactions with Ato. Perhaps this was so because El Yunque was my oasis. It wasn't Ato's or Mami's or anyone else's. It was mine.

Until Ato killed a little llorosa right in front of me. But Ato is gone now.

I banish the violent image from my thoughts and follow the familiar narrow path down to La Mina. Above me, giant tree ferns fan in the gentle wind. Moss blankets the trunks of the trees. I spot the brilliant white and green orchids and inhale their sweet fragrance. A small lagartijo runs out in front of my path but quickly disappears into a dense shrub. It is a winding path with so much to see, like these clusters of soft pink flowers. Impatiens. There they are like a tiny miracle. It's all here. El Bosque.

When I bend down to touch a dangling red hibiscus, the flower shrivels before my eyes, similar to how a morivivi, a plant native to Puerto Rico, closes its leaves when touched. But a hibiscus is not a morivivi.

I whirl around to see the rainforest destroying itself behind me. It is as if I am a virus contaminating everything with each step I take. In an instant, my joy dissolves into anger. This is yet another setting. Just like the house in the mountains and the river Ato re-created, so is this Yunque. It is a vision plucked from my mind only to be twisted and poisoned. He's gone too far this time.

I continue to walk toward the falls, each step fueled by hate. Behind me, I know that my precious Yunque keeps deteriorating, but I also know that it's not my fault. The water roars louder and louder until I reach the falls, where I notice a child sitting along the edge of a pool of water. She is crouched down, clutching her knees to her chest.

"What's wrong?" I ask the girl with thick, long hair.

She points to the sky, where a small patch of the sun's rays slipped through the foliage. I don't understand what she is afraid of. She begins to cry. Her tears fall into the pool of water. I bend down beside her and press my knees to my chest. In the distance, I can hear the sound of thunder. She begins to tremble. I, too, begin to tremble.

"They are coming back," she says in between cries. Her face is a river of tears.

"Who?" I ask the question, but I know the answer. I still need confirmation.

"The hurricanes. Don't you hear it?"

The thunder becomes louder. In the rainforest, there is no place to hide. We are vulnerable out here. Surely the winds will throw us into the pool of water, smash us against the falls. We will drown.

El Yunque dies around us in slow motion, and yet I can't move away from her. The mist turns into a heavy rain. It's hard to tell where our tears end and raindrops start.

"We have to go," I say. She is inconsolable. The young girl covers her ears with her hands.

"There's nowhere to run," she says.

I know this girl. She looks like me.

The waterfall stops churning as if someone turned a faucet off.

"Let's go," I tell her. Her wailing increases to match the thunder.

"You won't get far," the little girl says. "The island is meant to be destroyed."

I gasp. Her words are like punches. Puerto Rico is not a cursed island meant to be repeatedly ravished, be it from hurricanes or corrupt men or demented spirits. If I let her thought nestle into my bones, I will stay complacent. I will accept evil as something warranted. I know I don't deserve this, and neither does my home.

"No," I say. "This island is meant to just be. It flourishes despite everything natural and unnatural that tries to destroy it. I won't stay here and wait for the storm."

I try to grab her, but she refuses to come with me. El Yunque is being swallowed up, and she wants to stay. I won't.

Now that the falls have dried up, I can see an opening in the stone wall ahead of me. I head toward it, leaving the child behind. Around her, the rainforest continues to be wiped out.

I enter the opening in the mouth of the falls to find a set of stone steps. They lead down into a majestic Spanish courtyard. I can no longer hear the storm or the girl's cries. A woman stands at the bottom of the steps, offering me her hand. She is both beautiful and intimidating, and her hand feels like marble.

"You've arrived just in time," she says. "We've been waiting for you."

CHAPTER 33

Pheus

I'm not sure where to go. There's no map or sign. If my almost-drowning in the pool meant I crossed the bridge to el Inframundo, then Eury must be nearby. I hoist the guitar to my back and make my way off the cursed roof. It's completely dark, so pitch-black that I use my cell phone to illuminate the stairs. I take a deep breath and go.

A landing appears, one I'm sure wasn't there before. I pause and listen.

"Hello?" My voice echoes off the walls. Damn, do I keep going down, or do I cross the hallway? I wait. There is something out there, a slight sound of static like when a television stops working. I can barely hear it, but it's there. I walk toward the noise.

I sense I'm being watched, but I can't focus on who or what

lurks in these shadows. I hold tight to Eury's rosary and continue until I reach the end of the hallway where the static noise is louder. I stop in front of wooden double doors. Above the doors is a sign that reads Lecture Hall. Graffiti tags cover the brick walls. I push open the doors to find myself looking down at a large Spanish courtyard similar to the ones found on most Caribbean islands. Behind the courtyard is a two-tiered building with long white pillars and a surrounding balcony.

I locate where the static noise is coming from. On the far end of a wall, there are rows upon rows of computer screens. In front of the screens are men with long hair in spirals that plug into the sockets below the screens. Black men, Latinos, white men. Their fingers are also connected, and their eyes are white. They are causing the unearthly buzzing sound. It's as if these men are powering the computers with their energy.

It is only a short jump to the courtyard. When I land, the men don't move. I walk closer to see what's on the screens and immediately recognize the images and videos of Puerto Rico after the hurricane. The island in complete darkness. Those severest hit trying to find clean water to drink. Another cut, and I see the long lines for gasoline and the food rotting in containers instead of reaching the ones who need it the most. Hundreds of families left without their homes. Houses missing roofs. Elderly people trying to survive without their medication. Cut, and there is the racist president taking selfies with politicians, throwing things at residents who scramble to catch a roll of paper towels.

On another screen, white men talk about Bitcoins in front of landmark cathedrals in San Juan that have been converted into their offices. Their smiles are like vejigantes. They are part alligator and part human.

Other computer screens show medical experiments being done to Black and indigenous women. There is a screen of men's height being measured and their eyesight checked before being sent off to war. A man fighting in a boxing ring. A woman trying to feed her malnourished newborn. It goes on and on.

I quickly turn around, and a woman suddenly appears, seated in front of the two-tiered building on a regal wooden chair. Her face is furious. There is nothing delicate about her. Her arms stretch out like pillars. The hieroglyphics in the pamphlet from las casitas didn't do her justice. She is way more magnificent, way more terrifying. Guabancex, the Goddess of Chaos.

A man stands erect beside her, wearing a nagua and shells around his neck. His hair is inky black in a bowl cut, and his arms are as wide as a tree trunk. Dīs Pater. The God of Riches.

"Are you here to add to my collection?" Guabancex asks.

I wince. Her voice is roaring wind. It is surround sound,

as if hundreds of speakers are projecting her thunderous tongue.

I fall to my knees from the pain.

"I've come for Eury." I can barely get the words out, but I continue. "She's not meant to be here."

"You're not meant to be here, and yet, here you are."

The human computers begin to levitate. They go up and down like a perverse attraction.

"I've come to offer you a gift," I say. "A song to bring Eury back to earth."

Dīs Pater stands still and silent. For a second I wonder if he is even real.

"Do you know who I am?"

"Yes, you are the Goddess of Transformation, the Spiral in the Center, the . . . the . . ." I can't remember the rest of the greeting from the church pamphlet given to me by Doña Petra. Doña Petra, and everything from las casitas, feels like so many years ago. I stumble over my words and foolishly search for the piece of paper.

"I am the Cacique of the Wind, nonbeliever." Guabancex raises her long arms as if she is about to embrace a person. Instead, a violent gust of wind rises. "And I rule this place."

The wind picks me up and thrashes me across the court-yard. My guitar is lifted up to the sky and sent barreling down on me, smashing into pieces. The flurry sends me to the other side of the courtyard. I try to hold on to one of the pillars, my nails grating against the stone. It doesn't help. Soon another blast lifts me up into the air just like my guitar, and I am returned to the center.

I lie there for hours or minutes. I can't tell. Every single part of my body hurts. I'm bleeding from my nose. My lips are cut. Pants and shirt are torn up. It takes everything for me to get up, but I do. This storm won't stop me from delivering my present, from saving Eury.

"I've come to offer . . ."

My front tooth is loose and about to fall out. I try again.

"I've come to offer you a gift," I say. The pain is unbearable. I keep talking. "A song to bring Eury back to earth."

The goddess narrows her eyes, scrutinizing me. "I've seen your future."

The screens change to show my father at the park. His biker crew circles him. They are talking with concerned looks, consoling him. His face is gnarled in worry.

"A man who is unable to keep a job, let alone keep his family together," the goddess says. The wind picks up strength again but not as furiously as before. I am able to stand against it but not for much longer. "You're going to end up like him. Wishing you had taken another path. Regretting your choices."

I shake my head.

"No," I say. "My father has done his best."

"His best?" she says with a chuckle. "You don't even believe your own words."

The screen shows a close-up of my face as I turn away from my father while he argues on the phone with Mom. I can't even hide my disappointment.

"Perhaps you are right. But singers are such great seducers. Their voices are charm-inducing infusions," the goddess says. "Just ask Melaina."

Melaina appears on the screen. She stares at me while I sing at the beach. When my eyes focus on Eury, I see, for the first time, Melaina's heartbreak. Her sadness soon turns to anger. The screen flashes to another image. I'm with Melaina. I'm whispering in her ear. She giggles, but her eyes reflect how much she is suffering. Melaina knows this is the only affection I will give her, only the physical. She wanted more, and I didn't care.

"Stop," I say. The wind takes my words away.

"Eury was wrong in trusting you. You are not here for her. You are here because you crave the old myth of the hero galloping in to save the damsel," she says. "It's great to be loved, on that stage with all your adoring fans. Now *that* is what you truly want."

"I'm here for Eury," I say.

"Like so many others who roam the earth doubting what is right in front of them, you too are a skeptic. You do not deserve an audience with me," Guabancex says. "Cut his tongue out."

Dīs pulls out a glistening blade. The knife practically glows.

CHAPTER 34

Eury

Guabancex leads me to the courtyard where a magnificent woman sits on a wooden throne like royalty. Beside her stands a man just as menacing and fearsome.

"That's you," I say, pointing to the seated woman.

"Yes, it is," Guabancex says.

Her smile offers no comfort. I'm suddenly hit with the realization of how much I miss my mother. How far I am away from home and those who love me, stuck in an evil place where a god can appear in two places at the same time.

The seated goddess wages war on a boy. She sends his body flying with nothing but a breath.

"Pheus!" I scream.

"He overcame such obstacles and managed to cross

Charon's bridge because he wanted to save you. Aren't you impressed?" she says. "A knight traveling to the Underworld to be your savior."

"He doesn't deserve to be punished for it," I say. "Please, don't hurt him anymore. I beg you."

What can I do to save Pheus, to save us? Guabancex watches the spectacle of pain like it's a theater production. Pheus and I are not playthings. We are more than that.

I turn and face her.

"Let us go," I say with determination. "We traveled through this hell and still found a way to come together. Our love for each other led us here."

Out in the courtyard, the winds begin to pick up again. Pheus tries to stand, but he's losing strength.

"I am not here to only witness something as impractical as love. What matters is disorder," she says. "Chaos is where I find value. The unpredictability of humans. Case in point: Who would have thought the once-selfish Orpheus would have ventured to the Underworld in such a selfless act?"

The man in the courtyard pulls out a long knife. The goddess no longer negotiates with Pheus. What if all of this ends here?

No. This whole elaborate place is a set piece and el Inframundo is a large board game. We are pawns meant to entertain, and this game is not over.

"You won't kill Pheus because he still has enough fire in him to scorch this place to the ground," I say. "As do I. Together, we're unstoppable."

"You're quite the alchemist too," she says. "Aren't you, Ato?"

I don't have to turn around to know Ato stands behind me. I want to tear his face off. To grab the knife from the god in the courtyard and use it.

This is a form of cruelty, to present my abuser back to me. She is the Goddess of Chaos, and what she wants is unpredictability. I know my anger is exactly what she expects, but it's the only emotion I have right now.

"Let Ato take Pheus's place. Cut *his* tongue out instead."

She clucks, a surreal human reaction coming from a god. "Poor Ato. He believed in love too, just like your friend Pheus."

Love? Ato doesn't understand what love is. He is a parasite. I turn away from him, because ignoring him is the one thing that will eventually destroy him.

"Ato is not important," I say.

"Your eagerness to leave el Inframundo is misplaced," Guabancex says. "Those above are incapable of helping you. It is part of your lineage to wallow in misery. At least here you can live in paradise."

The goddess points to the computer screens. A young girl appears on one of them. Although it is daylight, she lies in her bed with the covers over her head. She's been crying. Her mother enters the room and drags her off the bed. She yells at the girl and forces her to hold a broom and a dustpan.

"I don't want to see you crying over una tontería. I'm tired of your laziness," the mother yells. "We don't have the luxury to be sad."

The girl does as her mother says, but her shoulders stay slumped. Whenever someone tries to address her, she can't meet their eyes. Those around her accuse her of pretending to be sad to get out of doing things.

The video jumps to another scene, and the girl is now a young woman. I've never seen Mami so beautiful with her long, flowing hair, but her face is pained. She rubs her belly, and I know I'm in there. She's on the phone, trying to explain how her sadness seems unbearable. But the person on the other end just yells. Mami begs for the person to understand, how she doesn't feel well. "I feel like a dark cloud presses down on me," she says. The person she talks to continues to reprimand her.

Another cut. My mother stares at the crib where I lie as if she is looking at a stranger. Papi is in the hospital with her. He tells her to hold me, but she doesn't want to. Papi doesn't understand. He says harsh words to her that make her cry. Mami tries to explain how she feels, but eventually she gives up. "How can you not love your own baby?" Papi asks. He cradles me until I fall asleep in his arms. Mami stares out the window, wiping her tears away.

I'm filled with such despair watching parts of Mami's life I've never seen before. Seeing her in such torment as a child. A depression no one understood. Not even her mother or her husband. I can't stop crying. Mami's suffering can't simply be wished away by prayers, but it is not a source of weakness. My family's legacy is not tied to hardship we must harbor inside of us like a rock.

"Your mother battles demons of her own," the goddess says. "At least in el Inframundo you would no longer be afflicted like her. Isn't that what you want? What your mother would want for you?"

I shake my head and try to stop myself from spiraling. El Inframundo isn't an antidote to what ails me because a gilded cage is still a cage. My poor mother. She only wants to help, but I can see how even Mami's suggestion to go to church and pray may have been wrong. But how can I fault her after seeing what she went through? My heart breaks for her.

"My mother only wants me to be well, and I want the same for her," I say in between sobs. "You show me only snippets of Mami's history, and perhaps they may be intertwined with mine, but we are not bound to them. El Inframundo isn't reality, and I was never given a choice."

I am running out of time. I dig deep within.

"Let me go so you can see how truly unpredictable my life

will be. All of us. Mami, Penelope. My aunt. Everyone. Pheus and I are products of a world where we are not meant to flourish, but we will. With every single obstacle put in front of us, we still persevere. We will thrive in spite of it."

Guabancex doesn't change her expression. She is stone, but I continue.

"I'm not meant to be alive, and yet here I am. We will show you," I say. "In the chaos you create, you will find our pattern of hope."

The god slowly walks to Pheus. The hand holding the knife is raised. He is about to strike. Pheus lifts his chin as if offering it to him. I hold my breath.

"Perhaps."

With that, the goddess in front of me vanishes. There is one goddess now, and she is still seated on the throne watching the fallen Pheus.

Let light shine over Pheus. Let grace guide us out of this place.

I pour my being into these sentences. I have only this faith to carry us.

CHAPTER 35

Pheus

The images on the screen continue to loop. My mother urging me to do better in math. My mother screaming at my father to get his shit together. Melaina brushing away tears. Cut to me playing up to the audience onstage like an asqueroso. The screens freeze on a close-up of my face leering at the girls in the audience like a lechón.

Guabancex is the director of this video compilation, and she's pleased with her work. She has seen me at my very worst and thinks that is the course I am destined to take. If ego drove me to the Underworld, love will surely lead me home. This is a fact.

Dīs Pater slowly makes his way to me. He raises his knife. If I'm meant to go, then I'm taking everything down with me. Everything.

Before Dīs Pater reaches me, I run over to the screens and the levitating bodies. I shove them out of my way. I don't look behind me to see what Dīs is doing, whether or not he's about to swing. I bash the screen with my fist and shatter it to pieces. Blood covers my knuckles. I keep going. Push the other computer screens to the floor. Kick them in.

"This is what I think of your videos!"

I ignore the pain in my hands. The cuts. The videos are ugly reminders that I've squandered my gift of music to manipulate others, like Melaina. I've treated it as a hobby and—because of fear—ignored Pops's advice to take my singing seriously. Pops always believed in my ability, but to consider this path meant to trust a man I was ashamed of. What did he know? He seemed lost, and I didn't want to be lost too.

But I'm not bound to these doubts, to this narrative. I can change.

When I am done destroying the screens, I stand before Guabancex. I'm torn up from my head down to my toes. There is nothing but pain. I settle my breathing and listen to the voice of my father telling me I am good, telling me I am blessed. I listen to Eury saying the same thing.

I have to give it one last try. I've made it this far. One last attempt to reach the celestial heavens and the depths of hell with a song.

The song I sing is the one I made for Eury. The lyrics have

a vulnerability boys like me, from the places I grew up, are not allowed to show. I bare it all because this song was meant to save us. Not just Eury, but me. To take me away from the roles I've forged. El amante. The player. The one to seduce the girls into doing what I want. Instead, I found Eury and finally dropped my dumb tiguere moves. The title of the song is "My Promise."

No more sweet lies. This heart only has room for Eury.
Una promesa de amor es la prueba.
No more playing el macho. This world can't contain her
    beauty,
Una promesa de amor que llega al alma.

Take this lament, we will bury it deep.
Take my hand, we will be created anew.
This I promise. This I promise.

No more denying what you see. Your words are truth.
Tus labios me encuentro, in this world and the next.
No more acting like I know. Time to walk in faith.
Tus brazos I fall for, mi verdadero amor will end this hex.

Take this lament, we will bury it deep.
Take my hand, we will create anew.
This I promise. This I promise.

When the song ends, I sing another, this time "Amorcito de Mi Alma" by José Manuel Calderón. I think of my parents and how they both want only the best for me. How I wish their love was enough. When I'm done, I continue with the song "Sombras Nada Más" by Javier Solís.

I lay it all out. I have nothing left to give.

Guabancex says nothing, but at least Dīs Pater puts away the knife.

The screens I destroyed slowly rebuild themselves. The shattered pieces, the holes I kicked in, fixed within minutes. The bodies stand up. They connect themselves right back to the machines. Everything returns to as before.

"How long have you known Eury?" Guabancex asks.

"I've known her all my life although we just met." I sound corny, and I can hear Jaysen ragging on me for stating such drivel. It's the truth, though. There are people I have crossed paths with before. This was something my father would say to me, and I would brush him off. If this place exists, so do other realms. Perhaps, in those other realms, Eury and I had met. It is possible. I know that now.

There is a silence that is almost defeating. The goddess and the god are still as statues. I wait.

"Because I am benevolent, I will let you escort Eury back upstairs."

I drop to my knees and cry. The emotions just pour out

along with my anxiety and anguish. I'm a mess, but I allow myself to feel this rawness without judgement.

She gestures with her hand across the courtyard, where an opening reveals the side of a hill, like any random hill you find in the Bronx. A reminder of what the Bronx must have looked like before buildings. A rural town where immigrants tried to carve a home.

"You have one minor obstacle to overcome," she says. "Eury will walk behind you. You will not hear her. She will be unable to touch you. If you turn around just once, she will stay here in el Inframundo forever."

Nothing is ever easy. One more obstacle to overcome.

"No problem," I say.

I can do this. She will be behind me, and I will guide her out of here. I don't care that I won't be able to see her. All that matters is that we leave and never return. We are so close. *Be safe. Don't be stupid.* Pops's words are forever at the forefront of my thoughts. They have guided me to this very moment. One simple task. To conjure up enough faith to walk us up the hill and straight home.

The goddess sighs.

"You remember Ato?" she says. He appears beside me out of nowhere. Anger courses through my veins. I've never wanted to kill as much as I want to dismantle whatever he is. Ato is the poison that contaminated Eury.

"Ato will help you along the way."

Ato stares at something, or someone, behind me. Then I know. He can see Eury, and I am not allowed to. He's once again granted access to her. This demonio. This evil.

Before I even know it, I am rushing toward Ato, toppling him down. Ready to pummel his face in.

"You piece of shit, whatever you are. When I leave this place, you are never to look for Eury again. You never deserved her friendship. You don't even deserve this right now."

"She loved me." He barely manages to speak in between my punches.

I stop. Ato looks even younger up close. What is age to him, though? He's a monster. A being that wears different masks. I saw his true colors, on the roof, minutes before Eury tripped and fell into the pool. His face wasn't human. What am I even doing wasting my energy on a lost spirit who will continue to roam this plane forever?

I get up. The problem won't be me trusting Eury is behind me. The problem will be having Ato here and not taking a stone to bash his head in.

"The interesting thing about Ato is how dedicated he is to Eury. The house he constructed was identical to the one on the island. He selected every little object for her. What devotion," Guabancex proudly says. "Ato, son of Night and Darkness. It took everything for him to be with Eury.

So many years spent waiting for the right moment. Didn't it, Ato?"

She caresses his cheek. I look away in disgust.

"Let's begin," the goddess says.

I face the hill, eager to start our ascent.

CHAPTER 36

Eury

"If you turn around just once, she will stay here in el Inframundo forever," Guabancex says.

As soon as she utters this, my body is placed behind Pheus. I stare at the back of Pheus's beautiful neck, and I want to kiss it. His broad shoulders I want to caress. But when I try to touch him, my hand goes through him like it's water. I am a ghost. He is right in front of me, and I am unable to communicate my love.

"This is cruel," I say to Guabancex, who continues to sit on her throne with a merciless grin plastered on her unworldly face.

"Don't worry. He won't travel completely alone," she responds.

Ato, the Spirit of Death, joins Pheus. He fixes his gaze on something past Pheus, trying to fool Pheus into thinking he can see me, but he can't. This is yet another trick, a final gamble to win the prize Ato spent so long yearning for.

"Why bring Ato into this?" I say. "Going up this hill is more than enough of a challenge."

Guabancex waves her unnatural hands to dismiss my statement.

"Ato and Pheus both want your heart," she says. "And I continue to be intrigued."

Ato continues the charade of seeing me. A liar until the very end, and I can't even muster anger for him. Rage won't change our circumstances. I need to funnel this energy into guiding Pheus in completing this last task.

"Pheus will fail," the goddess calls out from her throne.

"He won't fail," I say. I have enough faith for the both of us.

The Bronx is right at the top of the hill. We are so close.

"I'll see you soon," Guabancex says. Dīs stands scarily stoic beside her, forever her soldier. The goddess reverts her attention to the chaos televised on her many screens. There are new videos of graphic violence, unbelievable wealth, and disturbing poverty. It is an endless dance. What a spectacle our lives are to them.

Almost obscured in the far corner of the wall of screens

is a frozen image of Pheus and me grinning at each other. I hadn't noticed it before, but I do now. Our joy is also part of this chaos. Pheus and I will not succumb to their predictions. We won't.

Pheus begins to walk up the hill, and I follow.

CHAPTER 37

Pheus

I want to run. Hit that hill in no time, but I stop myself from doing so. Eury is behind me. We have to take this slow. I can't lose her again.

Ato walks alongside me. I want to push him away. Hurt him. I can't even pretend to ignore him. This is the thing. I'm jealous of Death because he still be winning. He can actually see Eury while I am stuck keeping my view steady on our destination. This whole ordeal began with him. It only makes sense the gods would continue this joke by having Ato with us until the very end, but what he doesn't know is that I aim to win.

"I remember your grandmother," Ato says. "The one who lived in North Carolina. Grandma Lynn."

He's actually going to do this. Ato's going to talk the whole way through. Try to trip me up. It's another test. I don't respond.

"Do you remember how right before she passed away, you said your goodbye?" Ato talks to me as if he's my boy, as if this is a conversation we were meant to have weeks ago and now is our chance to clear the air.

"Grandma Lynn didn't struggle. She knew it was time," Ato says. "When the time comes for your father, he will definitely struggle."

"Shut up."

"Your Pops is going to suffer for a long time," he says. "You will have to witness his painful demise and be unable to do anything to help him."

"Keep my father's name out of your mouth, Death. Whatever he has to go through, he will with a fight."

Eury is behind me. Remember this. I can't let Ato win.

"No, he doesn't believe me," Ato says. "Why do you think this will change? He will probably hurt you. Men don't change. Look at his father."

"Stop talking to Eury. She hates your guts just like I do."

The hill continues to ascend. It doesn't seem like we've made much progress, not with Ato yapping by my side. So, instead of engaging with him, I take a different approach.

"Eury, I'm going to tell you the story of when my parents met," I say.

I've always liked the story of when they first connected.

Perhaps it's just a child's foolish wish, but it always made me think of what can magically happen when two people meet. Perhaps if I recite this story, I can drown out Ato.

Ato continues to talk. He speaks about my father's death. I won't listen. I see Eury's face in my mind's eye and focus on that, like I'm talking to only her.

"My parents met in college. They were both young and optimistic. Basically, my father swore he was cool. He could easily talk to girls, but there was this one sister who refused to give him any play. Moms was too smart. Too fly. Too everything, and she knew it. So when Pops rolled up on her and tried to use his smooth words, she wasn't having it. She shot him down every single time."

Death speaks louder. He now talks about Eury's mom and how she will die. We will not let him win.

"It wasn't until Pops stopped trying so hard that Mom finally gave him some attention. They were at a house party and their group of friends was arguing over who was the best guitar player. Pops listened mostly to merengue and salsa. Not Mom. Moms knew the names of all the greats— Jimi Hendrix, B.B. King, Howlin' Wolf. Pops was in awe. When the time came to go, Pops ran up to Moms and said, 'I don't know much about strings, but I've heard he's one of the best. Do you like this song?' It was Prince's 'The Beautiful Ones.' Back then, everyone was singing 'Purple Rain,' but Pops loved the lyrics to 'The Beautiful Ones,' and so did Mom."

Damn. I completely forgot how Prince brought my parents together. One song. How powerful is that? Pops always said that there are no coincidences. I can see that now. Music can be the conduit, the bridge. I have proof of this because I met Eury. Our love crossed dimensions and music was our guide to salvation. It was fate. I was meant to meet Eury, and we are destined to walk this hill together.

Ato finally shuts up. He stares at the ground, like his sadness is weighing him down.

"There was a time I thought if I learned how to sing the song, I could make them remember the night they fell for each other. Ridiculous, huh? Maybe that's why Mom has never been that keen on me playing the guitar."

I almost turn around, expecting Eury to be smiling, reaching out to me with a simple gesture like laying her hand over mine. What I would do to feel that right now. I continue.

"I guess when you're young, you fail to see the reality of life. The choices my parents made. I don't know. I still wish things were different between them," I say. "Music can move mountains, but it couldn't save my parents' marriage or my father from depression."

Is it weird I can almost sense Eury reprimanding me for being such a bummer? We draw closer to the top of the hill.

Ato is still buried deep in his thoughts. Let him stew in that forever. All I can think of is how tight I will hold Eury once we reach the top. There's so much for us to talk about. A real future to plan ahead for.

Almost there. I can feel it. Taste it even. This nightmare will soon be behind us.

"She doesn't want to continue," Ato says.

I stop. He stares behind me.

"She keeps screaming no," he says. "She's afraid."

"What do you mean she's afraid? What's going on?"

I have to look. What if she's in pain?

"She can't go on."

"Eury! Talk to me. Send me a sign. I can't look back. If I do, it's done. Please!"

What do I do?

CHAPTER 38

Eury

"I remember your grandmother. The one who lives in North Carolina . . ."

Ato is a seducer. Isn't that what Death does? Death promises to end the suffering. Ato hopes Pheus will be lured. Because I have no other weapon, I speak to Pheus and beg him not to listen.

"Don't let him take us down," I say.

Pheus is able to resist for now. He talks to me, and I listen to how his parents met. How "The Beautiful Ones" brought them together, just like Prince did for us. We are so near. I can see the sky opening up. Our future is a few steps away.

Ato is gripped with anguish. He also sees how close we are to ending his deadly chase forever. So Ato changes course.

"She doesn't want to continue," he says. "She keeps scream-ing no. She's afraid."

"He's lying!" I scream.

There is a slight smirk on Ato's face that only I can see. "What do you mean she's afraid? What's going on?" Pheus is panicking. I can sense his faith leaving him.

"She can't go on," Ato says.

"Eury! Talk to me. Send me a sign. I can't look back. If I do, it's done. Please!"

"Don't listen to him," I say. "Please, Pheus, listen to your heart. He is a liar. He only wants to keep me trapped here. Ignore him."

If Pheus turns back, he will lose me forever. One glance is all it takes. Pheus stops walking. He has to keep going. We are nearly there. The atmosphere has changed. We are leav-ing this realm. Can't he feel it?

Ato pretends to talk to me. Like Pheus, he can't hear or see me, and yet he continues to fool Pheus.

"Please, Pheus, keep going. Forget about Ato and take another step."

I try to push him, but my hand goes right through him.

"She's doubled over," Ato says. "If she goes any farther, it's only going to get worse. Didn't the goddess warn you of this?"

Pheus is unsure of what to do.

Don't turn back. What Guabancex said was true. I will be rooted in this plane forever.

"Tell her I have her rosary right here. Can you tell her?" Pheus shoves it in Ato's face. Ato shakes his head as if it won't matter. How easy was it for him to deceive me all those years? To pretend to be my age, to be my coconspirator. The hate I have for him can engulf entire worlds.

If only Pheus would look ahead, he would see how the hill turns into the streets he is so familiar with. New York is within reach. His home. And beyond that, my sweet island, waiting for me to return. We are not meant to be here. There is too much work to do, too much life to live. Can't he see how close we are?

"You have to help her," Ato says with such concern that for a brief moment I check to make sure I am still okay.

"How? I can't turn back. Tell me how."

Pheus grabs Ato by the shoulders. Ato even tears up as if he is heartbroken.

I look around, desperately trying to find something to help me. We're so close! A couple more steps and we are free. My vision blurs as tears overflow from my eyes.

"Eury wants me to tell you she's meant to stay here. If she crosses over, she'll die. She is sorry."

My hands shake with rage. How can Pheus so quickly forget Ato's only want? How can Pheus be the most brave and still be the most insecure? It's only a matter of time before he breaks.

"Pheus. Remember when you texted me this verse from

the Bible, 'Do not let your hearts be troubled. You believe in God, believe also in me.' Believe in yourself, in what is true," I say. "We are inches away from life, and you stand here trusting Death."

"You have to turn around before it's too late. She's sick," Ato cries. "Only you can save her!"

"Believe in yourself." An incantation to somehow reach Pheus. I continue to recite it like a prayer, over and over.

"I got to help her," Pheus says.

This is it. A tidal wave is about to wash over me, and I wait for it to tear me apart.

Slowly, Pheus turns to face me. I reach for his hand.

My beautiful Pheus.

"Mi amor," I say to him.

I feel the warmth of his fingers until I no longer do.

CHAPTER 39

Pheus

"Son."

I follow the voice. It sounds familiar although distant. There is noise. People are talking. My eyes slowly adjust to the lightbulb shining from above. I've come to on the floor of the Casita Rincón.

Pops kneels before me, handing me a glass of water. I take a slight sip, only enough to be able to say her name.

"Eury."

The memories return. The jawless servers. Charon and his machete. Guabancex and Dīs Pater. The hill and the proposition, and Ato telling me how Eury was in pain. But most of all, I remember Eury's face and her hand in mine before she turned to dust.

Pops shakes his head. He's not going to tell me, is he? How

I failed. I traveled to el Inframundo and returned without her. No. I don't care what rules I broke. This story can't end here. It can't.

"Where is she?" I get up. She's not gone. She can't be.

"I'm sorry," Doña Petra says with tears in her eyes.

I run as fast as I can, practically knocking people out of the way in las casitas. Eury can't be gone. Her hand was in my hand. Warm. She was real. We touched for a second, and it was right. I don't care what the goddess said, the deal she made with me. Eury was alive with me on top of the hill. We made it out of there together.

The waiting room in the hospital is filled with people. They are crying and holding each other. Jaysen is the first to see me. He wears the same clothes from the night before. Then again, so do I, although I feel as if I've been gone for weeks. Jaysen leans in to give me a hug. I push him away.

"Is she still in the same room?" I say.

"They moved her. It doesn't look good. Her body's not responding, bro," Jaysen says. He's choked up. "I'm sorry, Pheus."

My crew surrounds me. They try to hold me back, as if that's even possible.

"Get off me and just point me to where she's at!"

Jaysen finally hears me.

"Room six. She's in room six."

Eury's room is filled to capacity. Penelope is being held by her mother. A woman kneels by Eury, and I immediately see the resemblance. Eury's mom. And then there is Eury lying on the bed. *Eury.* She's connected to even more tubes than before. The machines beep their uncomfortable music.

"Pheus, you need to leave right now," Penelope says. "You can't be here."

"Oh, you're Pheus?" Eury's mom says, standing and shaking in grief and fury. "You were the one who took her to the club, and now she's here. It's because of you she's suffering!"

Penelope's father tries to hold her, but she is still able to slap my face. She has every right to be angry. She doesn't know how many times I failed her daughter.

Before I am thrown out of the room, I go to Eury and place my hand over hers. I didn't expect to feel such coldness. It breaks me.

"Eury, I wasn't smart enough. I . . ." Words are useless in conveying my grief. My failure. But what else can I do but plead for her to find her way out of that hell? I have only these pitiful sentences.

Penelope cries.

"Sir, you need to leave right now." A man in a nurse's uniform places a firm hand on my shoulder. He is big and burly, but I'm not moving. He might as well start using his muscle because I'm staying put.

"This is yours," I say and place the rosary around Eury's fingers where it belongs. "Eury, you are stronger than me. Come home to us."

There is a grand commotion, and I am in the center of it. Security piles into the already crowded room. They yank at me. I clutch the side of the bed.

"Let go!" They got three brothers on me. I push, kick. Do whatever I got to do to stay, all the while suplicando a Eury.

"Get him out of here," someone yells.

The men have plied my hands from the bed. They have me by the door, ready to toss me out.

I shut my eyes and pray to Guabancex. Implore her. "Guabancex, please hear me. Let Eury bring forth goodness. Let her offset this cruel world with hope."

They are pushing me out the door, away from Eury. I keep praying.

CHAPTER 40

Eury

I feel hollow, as if my insides have been drained away and I am only a husk. It was never meant to be easy, this test, and yet I thought Pheus would pass. I had faith in him. My heart is already broken in so many pieces, but I'm numb to this new agony.

"He was never going to make it up the hill," I say. "The test was fixed for him to fail."

Pheus and Ato no longer stand before me. They are gone, and the only person here is Guabancex.

"It was a simple enough rule to follow," the goddess says. "And yet he was unable to listen to a woman, a god no less."

Guabancex placed my life in the hands of a boy who just the other day said he only trusted in the tangible. Pheus learned so much in so little time, but it wasn't enough. The goddess condemned Pheus's lack of trust while she coddled Ato. Her rules are like water.

"This wasn't a true test. It was just an excuse to show how flawed humans are." I'm so tired of this circular argument I can't seem to break free from. Any sliver of hope I've been clinging to all this time slowly erodes. What more can I do?

"Come, let's take one last stroll," Guabancex says. I follow her along the quiet Bronx streets. It is early morning, and the few people walking near us are oblivious to our presence.

"So much construction. Soon this place will be unrecognizable," she says, pointing to the new buildings and the old tenements being destroyed. "Dīs Pater continues to thrive. It's so impressive."

Although my heart aches for my short time on earth, she's wrong to see only this side of the Bronx. There is more than just new developments meant to displace those who have lived here for so long. I point to a young mother gently pushing a child on a swing. The baby giggles each time.

"That is way more powerful than anything Dīs Pater creates," I say. "And that."

I point to an older woman setting up her coquito stand by the train station. A family walking together. A man wishing another man a good morning.

"These small inklings of joy aren't enough," the goddess says. "Most humans prefer to lean toward the promise of wealth. Waging war on each other to prove their dominance.

I've seen this displayed on my many screens time and time again."

"You are wrong. For so long, I could only see darkness, always waiting for evil to come for me. I forgot what true happiness was until recently," I say. "I forgot there is beauty everywhere, and I am worthy of it. Me."

We continue to walk. I pause to watch a young girl cross herself as she passes a church. She smiles at an old lady and asks for her blessing. I let the goodness around me fill me with light.

"Pheus was never meant to rescue me," I say. "I was always meant to save myself. I overtook Sileno at the club. I did that. And I was the one who escaped Ato, not Pheus. Me, by myself. Place me right before Death again, and I will do the same."

The goddess continues to walk, but I grab her arm. It is as hard and cold as marble. I have nothing to give to her, nothing left to prove. Either she sends me back to el Inframundo or she lets me go.

"No more of these so-called tests. I'm way too smart for them, and you know it," I say. "You are bored with your television channels full of despair. It's time to change your view."

We've stopped in front of a large brown building. An ambulance pulls into the driveway.

"There is so much unrest on earth, both good and bad. I simply nudge from one direction to another. People choose the next step while I sit back and watch how the disorder unfolds. It has always been this way," the goddess says as she faces the building. "Revolutions and agitations. Extreme highs and the unrelenting drops. Love and heartache. I see it all."

She turns to me.

"So, tell me, what type of havoc will you bring?"

"The best kind," I say, but I am cut off as Guabancex causes the building to flip upside down. The street is now the sky. Or is it my body that's in motion? I am floating, and I don't know which direction I am going. I close my eyes. Soon enough my destination will reveal itself, and whether I am in el Inframundo or back home, it will be a battle to survive. But I am ready.

I hear shouting and beeping noises. The voices sound familiar. I concentrate hard until I am certain I can reach them.

The security guards have got a hold on me. I dig my nails into the hospital door. Penelope's father joins in on the ruckus to throw me out, but I keep holding on. Keep praying.

"You've done enough damage to this family," he says. He's itching to throw a punch. I brace myself for the hit.

"Wait!" Penelope screams. "Wait! Look. Look at her."

Everyone stops. The nurse. The security guards. Penelope's father. Me.

We turn to Eury. Her eyes flutter. We collectively hold our breath. The room is still. No, the whole world is still.

Eury slowly opens her eyes and blinks, scanning the room before settling on my face.

"Pheus," she says, and it's more than enough.

In fact, it's everything.

CHAPTER 42

Eury

"Are you packed?" he asks.

The beach is crowded. Penelope and Aaron walked off to buy something at the kiosk. It's almost time for lunch. The sun is hidden behind large clouds. There is a slight threat of rain. Penelope wanted to cancel today's outing, but I convinced her not to.

"Almost," I say.

Pheus sits on the cooler and tunes his new guitar. Jaysen swears up and down it was donated by an anonymous fan who saw Pheus perform at Dīs-traction. Pheus doesn't believe him. He thinks Jaysen forced the owner, Sileno, to cough up the dough. I also heard they did other things to him too, worse than just forcing him to open his wallet. Pheus didn't press for details, and neither did I.

I look over Pheus's application for the music program on a borrowed iPad. I'm reading his essay, which he titled "The History of My Lamentations." He writes about bachata music and its connection to the Dominican Republic. How this music has traveled from an island to this city. My favorite part is when he breaks down the lyrics to his song, the one he performs in the video he's sending in. My song.

I'm sure Pheus will be accepted into the program. The only obstacle will be convincing his mother to go along with it.

"What time is your flight?"

"You've asked me that three times already." I laugh. "We leave early tomorrow. Mami wants to get me on a schedule. My first appointment is on Monday."

In the past few weeks, I've met with a therapist. It was scary at first, speaking to a stranger. A part of me understands how it will help, and another part still feels I must stick to hiding my problems. But I like her. She's Panamanian and has a calm demeanor, one free of judgment. Convincing Mami to let me see her hasn't been easy. But two days after I woke up, we sat down and spoke. It was so hard to be honest with her. She didn't want to hear about my torment and how I can no longer continue on my own.

"All you need is faith in God," she said as she tried hard to contain her emotions.

"That's not enough, Mami. I need both faith and professional help," I said. "I've been sad for so long, ever since Papi left. And after what happened during the hurricane, I need to find a way of dealing with my anxiety. I don't know how to do it by myself."

She shook her head. "They're going to give you drugs, and you won't be the same person." I recalled the images of her so young, hiding under the covers, unable to cope. I wished I could tell her what I saw. Instead, I tried again.

"We need help to deal with this heaviness. Don't you feel it?" I said. "I felt it in Puerto Rico and in Florida. I don't want to continue carrying this. We can find a therapist who can understand where I'm coming from, perhaps someone from the island. Please, Mami, let's try."

The conversation lasted a long time. There were many tears. Mami is scared. So am I. But I can see Mami's opinion shifting, and that gives me hope. It's not a complete one-eighty, but it helps that the therapist speaks Spanish. We have appointments to see someone in Florida too. It's a big step, for both of us.

Pheus stops fiddling around with his guitar and smiles at me.

I haven't seen or heard from Ato. My vigilance is still very much real. At the first sign of rain, the shakes begin, then the cold sweats. My instinct is to hide. To run. Even while I sit here, I can't help but keep careful watch of the increasing clouds. The therapist should be able to help me with this. It will take time, but I'm ready to take it.

"Hey," Pheus sits beside me. "What can I do?"

The issue isn't the lack of help from the people who care for me. Sometimes the answer isn't a simple statement. Do this and I will feel better. Say this word and I will return to acting "normal." There is no such thing as normal or a magical fix. Solutions can be found in a combination of things—talking to a therapist, medication, and incorporating tips to help with my anxiety. It's hard for Pheus. As with history, he thinks he can predict the outcome.

What is the opposite of predictability?

"Keep playing the guitar."

He leans in and pecks my cheek. Pheus hasn't left my side, even after Penelope's father threatened to kick his ass. After a while, my family accepted him.

Jaysen arrives, talking loudly on his phone. The others are not too far away. Melaina and her friends. Conga players. They want Pheus to join them. He hasn't committed. Jaysen has been traveling between both camps, trying to keep everyone happy.

"A sweet sixteen party in September. What do you think? The pay isn't much, but it's a start. Plus, they want to livestream the whole thing."

"'Chacho, ¿tú no paras?" Pheus asks, slightly annoyed.

"Can't stop. Won't stop," Jaysen says. "Besides, I'm sure Eury wants to see you performing. Keep an eye on you. Make sure you on key. Am I right?"

Each night, Pheus plays a song for me. He has been trying to translate the lyrics to Prince's slow jams into Spanish. Change them up into a bachata. We've spent hours going over one song, and I still don't think it's quite right. Pheus thinks I'm too much of a perfectionist, but verses are not meant to be so literal. Symbolism is way more important.

I sweep my curtain of hair to one side. Although the sun is hidden, it is still very hot.

Penelope and Aaron soon return.

"Prima, can you braid my hair?" I ask. Penelope sits behind me, her knees pressing against me. Facing the ocean, she takes her time. My hair is so long.

"Remember when I used to do this for you when we were kids?" she says. "You were my practice."

"I cried that one time when you pulled my hair way too hard."

"That was because you didn't want to share your coconut candy with me."

"Mala." I nudge her. Penelope promises to come visit me for Thanksgiving. Tampa isn't too far away. I wish I could take them all with me in my luggage, especially Pheus.

The plan is for Mami and me to go to Puerto Rico for Christmas with Penelope and her family. I know it's asking too much for Pheus to join us as well. Besides, he will be busy with school and other obligations. There is no money for a trip.

I have my own intentions, things I want to do. Besides

taking care of myself, I want to find a way to return to the island. It's why Mom and I are visiting for Christmas. Florida doesn't feel right, and neither does the Bronx. I've started to think of what I want to do after high school, what I want to do in Puerto Rico. For the first time in a long time, I am thinking of the future. My ideal life is not fully fleshed out in my head, but there is the hint of possibility. What will Puerto Rico become for me? I get to shape what that looks like. Although I'm afraid, I'm also excited.

Pheus's father came to visit me in the hospital and gave me a book: *Puerto Rico mío*, a collection of photographs by a famous photographer, Jack Delano. On the cover is a close-up of a young girl who is about eight years old. There is something about her that reminds me of Ato. A sadness in her eyes. At first, I didn't want to accept the gift because the resemblance seemed too real. Too painful.

"You have to know your history before you can move forward," he said. "Some people say dwelling in the past can be a crutch, but you can't ignore it either. There has to be a fine balance."

I thanked him for the book. It really is a beautiful tribute to my home. Pheus says his father is still working with the movers and still pining for his mother. This is a topic that hurts Pheus, but he is trying to accept it.

"How long before you sing a damn song?" Jaysen says, loud enough so the families near us laugh along.

Pheus rolls his eyes. He plucks a fast bachata on his guitar, one meant to be danced close to your partner. The song he sings is "Donde Estará," by Antony Santos. A song of a man looking for his woman, asking where his "dulce mujer" is.

As soon as he starts, Penelope and Aaron get up. Their bare feet shuffle against the sand. Aaron is a great dancer. He learned over the summer as a way to draw Penelope closer to him. She loves it.

"C'mon, Eury."

Jaysen grabs my hand, and we join in on the dancing. Like his talking, Jaysen's moves are choppy and quick. He spends most of the time twirling me around, which is difficult on the sand, but we manage. With each spin, I search for Pheus. His laughter makes him miss a verse, so he begins again. No one seems to mind.

Pheus sings another song, and we keep dancing. The other families listen. A baby in diapers starts jumping up and down, and his family takes a video of it. He is pure joy.

After a third song, I am completely out of breath. No more dancing in circles. My head is still not right, what with the stitches.

Jaysen starts dancing with the mother of the baby. My stomach hurts from laughing.

If only this could last forever. I concentrate and take a mental picture of how Pheus's fingers pull at the strings of the guitar. How he leans forward when he wants to emphasize a verse. How Penelope squeals every time Aaron turns her. How the baby claps his tiny hands together. He has found his own rhythm.

When Pheus stops, the small crowd cheers and thanks him.

From across the way, we hear rap music pulsing from a speaker.

"Yo, they playing the new one."

Jaysen goes back to the other section, promising to return in a bit.

"We will be back." Penelope and Aaron join Jaysen, wanting to keep the dance party going.

I lie on my back. There is another dark cloud joining the others. Will it be enough to make it rain? I practice my breathing exercises.

With Pheus beside me, the anxiety quells but only slightly. He is not my medicine. I have to figure this out on my own, and that is not a bad thing. Instead of facing the sky, I turn my body toward him. He does the same.

"Aaron said he'll drive me to the airport. We'll follow your uncle's car."

I knew he would figure out a way to prolong this goodbye.

I search for his hands. His rough fingertips lightly caress my skin. Our fingers intertwine.

When I close my eyes, I can see us both back on my island. My house is still intact. The llorosas are up in the tree. Each branch taken over by the tiny birds. They keep us company, vigilant over us. In this vision, Pheus and I are eager to see what we will discover. All around us, families are rebuilding. There is an outpouring of energy, excitement for what's to come.

Pheus tugs at my hand.

"Hey," he says, lightly kissing my forehead. "Where did you go?"

"Not far," I say. "I will describe it so you, too, can see what I see."

He closes his eyes. I lean on him and whisper this vision of us in his ear.

ACKNOWLEDGMENTS

As I sit down to write this, the National Guard has set up shop a block away from my home in response to uprisings against police brutality, while an uncurable pandemic surges. Our present is disturbingly uncertain. Three years ago, I grappled with how trauma seeps into the fabric of each generation. *Never Look Back* emerged from this with Pheus and Eury, two characters that embody what so many young people deal with on a daily basis: How to love and thrive when the world is set against you?

Never Look Back is also about the stigma behind mental health therapy. According to the American Association of Suicidology, Latinas have had among the highest rates of depressive symptoms and suicide rates compared to other groups for over thirty years, but only one in eleven Latinas ever seek treatment. My depression and anxiety have followed me since I was a child but it took me years to finally seek professional help. If you are struggling today, please call the National Suicide Prevention Lifeline at 1-800-273-8255. You are not alone.

So many people helped make this novel possible. Thank you so much to my editor Claire Stetzer and the wonderful team at Bloomsbury. Thank you to the Bronx-raised, Puerto Rican artist Krystal Quiles for creating such a beautiful cover. Thank you to Adriana M. Mártinez Figueroa for providing such an insightful sensitivity read. Thank you to my agent Eddie Schneider who read the first draft and urged me to keep going. Thank you to bachata, Prince, Gluck's opera *Orphée et Eurydice*, and the movie *Black Orpheus*. And thanks to Puerto Rico, the island that always inspires.

When Hurricane Mária destroyed so many living on the island, including my family, I sought a way to funnel my rage and hopelessness. The Greek myth of Orpheus and Eurydice was the structure I needed to tell this tale of young love and hope. My wish is that you find a little bit of both on these pages.